The
Boarder

The
Boarder

A novel

Jane E. Ryan

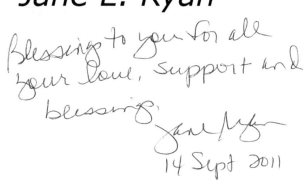

Blessings to you for all
your love, support and
blessings.
Jane Ryan
14 Sept 2011

iUniverse, Inc.
New York   Bloomington

The Boarder

A Novel

iUniverse books may be ordered through booksellers or by contacting:

iUniverse
1663 Liberty Drive
Bloomington, IN 47403
www.iuniverse.com
1-800-Authors (1-800-288-4677)

ISBN: 978-1-4502-0232-9 (pbk)
ISBN: 978-1-4502-0233-6 (ebk)
ISBN: 978-1-4502-0234-3 (hbk)

Printed in the United States of America

iUniverse rev. date: 12/29/09

DEDICATION

During a discussion about the relationship with her young, highly disturbed son, a victim of Reactive Attachment Disorder, the mother said her boy was like a boarder in a boardinghouse of yesteryear.

The sad, bewildered woman stated,"They live in your house and eat at your table, but you never really know who they are."

Out of love and respect for all the Boarders on our paths, this book is dedicated to children traumatized early in their lives, to those who will be abused in the future, and to the brave souls who fight to love and return them to us.

Please, God, bless us all.

The Boarder...

...is a fictionalized story
inspired by true life experiences
lived by generous families who,
out of abundant love in their hearts,
unknowingly opened their homes and lives
to disturbed children.

ACKNOWLEDGEMENTS

I am full of gratitude to my children – GDL, JRL, LAL and PDL – for sharing a portion of their childhoods with me. It was through a combination of the pleasure and the pain from those early years that this volume was eventually born.

I have deep feelings of gratitude for the love given me by my mother Joyce Carlisle Ryan, and sisters Suzanne Inciong, Kathleen Martin, Patricia Ryan and Julia Ryan, along with Katie Ishol and my other magnificent Step Sisters in Hawaii and Nebraska.

Along the way the lovely Valerie West helped me remember that I really can do anything I am able to dream. Many thanks to Merlene Paul, Beverly Morgan, Marianne Kiskola, and Christena Baker for loving me just the way I am. And a very special thanks to my editor Suzanne for making this project look so good and to Sharon Loy and the fine people of Ravenna, Nebraska for not laughing when I laid some of my most grandiose ideas on them.

But the greatest gratitude goes to my higher power, humbly called 'The Big Guy,' who has gifted me with an amazing life that is far beyond my comprehension. When I finally learned that all I had to do was to follow a few suggestions, my life as I knew it changed completely. And even with a voracious imagination that I must feed regularly, my life has become far better than I could ever imagine or deserve.

I am certain of few things in life, but I do know that any creative gifts I have to give to the world come through me and have always been from HIM.

Dear God,

Thank you for listening to my prayers and for giving me the courage to pick up a pen while I waited for Your answers. I am yours.

JER

It is one of those spring days that sucks breath from your chest, entices you to draw air deep into your lungs and fills you with the hope of new promise all in the same, indescribable moment. The gently rolling hills west of Lincoln are lush with the thick, deep green growth of lavender–tipped alfalfa. The new corn plants, already nearly a foot high, look as if the Maker has attached miniature lights to the underbelly of each succulent, tiny leaf. From the sky, field after field of new corn bumping up against the robust alfalfa looks like a bright green shiny carpet that's been nourished by recent Midwestern thunderstorms.

Heaven high, puffy clouds are at first white, luminescent, and in the process of turning to shades of dark, grayish black. Within minutes ominous clouds, pregnant with a pending downpour, like those commonly seen at the end of hot, steamy days, appear on the horizon. Herds of Angus and Hereford cattle, accustomed to heart-stopping claps of thunder followed by jagged patterns of lightning that rip across the expansive sky, graze undisturbed.

In the blink of an eye storms of such power and fury fill the open spaces, startling strangers new to the region. Thrilled by the unpredictability of the event, mixed with the overwhelming smell of rain and the scent of sweet corn blanketing rolling hills, spring is heralded through middle America. Undaunted by the downpour, tall, gray-white grain silos remain stalwart and silent, awaiting their season and the variety of crops. Fall harvests highlight grain collections made by small family farms now dot the Nebraska landscape.

From the crest of a hill near the Crete interchange the golden dome of the State Capitol building, precarious home of the golden "Sower," juts from the level floor of the plains. Although awesome in its monolithic splendor, it serves as a reminder of the power and pride of a city considered sleepy and insignificant by those who simply pass by.

The University of Nebraska football stadium, an imposing structure that sits majestically at the edge of downtown Lincoln, is a monument to countless successful missions. Even when empty, if you lean toward that hallowed ground and listen carefully, you can hear the remnants of the wild cheers of red-clad fans and ghosts of football seasons past.

Even though it's a city of nearly one quarter of a million people, Lincoln is still much like a "cow town grown up" as old residents claim. Now it is the fourth largest relocation center for refugees from poorer countries of the world, including many African and Asian peoples. Because of the influx, the population of the Nebraska capital has become more colorful, increasingly complex, and more cosmopolitan than most outsiders realize.

As one travels through the tidy, increasingly congested streets, a variety of impressive yet older neighborhoods present themselves. Some still represent the majesty of bygone days with their Victorian gingerbread and wrap-around porches. Others just down the street are in a poorer state of repair, and now serve as transitional homes for young families or recent immigrants to the area.

The perimeter of an ever-expanding city shows signs of new things to come. Noisy earth movers busily finish palatial homes that are springing up like great walls surrounding the city, signaling a new era filled with economic promise.

A multitude of churches, homes to countless denominations and cultures, have stately spires that can be seen from above as they pierce the thick green canopy present throughout the city. The harmonious sounds of church bells and holy chimes soften the imposing shrill of train whistles, the rhythmic clacking of steel wheels on steel rails. The sounds of industrial commotion are muted by the collection of church choirs that send messages to the heavens, perhaps reminders of holier, more saintly times.

Without straining, one can hear the voices of gospel choirs throughout the city warming up and preparing for the next day's glorious performances.

⮞ 2 ⮜

In the lateness of the night, neon lights and rhythmically blinking stoplights cast eerie shadows on the nearly empty streets of Lincoln. Hand-in-hand, a few couples wander aimlessly around downtown drawing little attention to their silent activities. The clock in the Wells Fargo Bank window claims it's two a.m. as occasional youthful drivers whip past vacant shops and squeal their tires as they interrupt the late night peace.

Officer Sullivan, as heavily muscled and toned as a thirty-four-year-old weight lifter can get, drives his black and white police cruiser slowly along "O" Street. His eyes are sharp and alert as he purposefully peers into the dark nooks and hooded doorways. Tall, intense twenty-something Officer Newell, Sullivan's backup, uses his spotlight so he can see into the many crannies along the alleyways behind area businesses.

Finding nothing, Sullivan crosses the intersections of Fourteenth and Fifteenth Streets methodically checking for his unseen quarry. Radio static in the background reminds both officers of their perpetual tether to the force behind them.

Officer Sullivan leans his head toward his right shoulder and talks softly into a nearly invisible microphone strapped to his shoulder. "See him yet?" he nearly barks into the mic.

"Nope. I thought I had him earlier, but that little shit is so sneaky. And fast," replies Newell to his partner.

Perhaps junking up the airwaves, Officer Sullivan complains, "This is getting mighty old. You'd think there would be at least one place in this entire town that's secure enough to keep him locked up tight."

Suddenly, Newell spots movement and speeds down the alley before him. At the intersection he steps on the gas and turns sharply on to a road that takes him the wrong way down a clearly marked one-way street. Cursing under his breath, the vigilant officer takes a moment to look up to the skies and say a quick thanks for no traffic at this time of night.

With no idea of hiding his excitement, Newell shouts into his radio, "I've got him! He's running north on Sixteenth. Go north around the block. We're going to nail him this time!"

Sullivan, who has built a reputation on being up for the chase and a little risky behind the wheel, grins as he drives Dukes-of-Hazard style through a parking lot and onto the street. The officers meet in the middle of the road where they box in a small, wiry figure between their overheated cruisers.

Newell gingerly leaps from a barely stalled black and white with Sullivan on his heels. Officer Newell grabs the arm of the dirty youth and roughly shoves him up against the patrol car.

"Gotcha!" the officer exclaims with a little too much glee.

Officer Sullivan enjoys his own sense of humor and with drawn out, exaggerated pleasure says, "Well, hello, Carl."

Carl is tall for his age and the officers know he's only eleven, but in some areas of his life he's going on thirty-five. The kid is his usual surly self and challenges the officers.

Carl snarls, "Let me go, you fuckers! It's past your curfew and your mamas want you home."

With a mixture of enjoyment and tart humor, Sullivan responds, "Still cute after all this time. Right, Carl? How many times have we had to pick you up so far?"

While trying to escape the officers' vice-like grips, Carl shrugs and sneers, "I dunno. I can outrun you so this won't be the last, I'm sure of that."

Both officers work together in their attempt to cuff the writhing, adrenaline-filled youth. When finally under control, Carl is stuffed in the back seat of Newell's patrol car. Because of Carl's history and determination to get free, Newell is a little paranoid about losing him. All the way to the Juvenile Hall Newell keeps a close eye on his struggling charge locked in the back seat.

The younger officer speaks to the dispatcher waiting for word on the other end. "I'm taking Carl Johns to the Detention Center. Guys, give them the heads up that they need to hang on to him this time around. Okay?"

Dispatch replies wryly, "What a good idea! This kid reminds me of that old song, something about thieves in the night."

Confined in a cruiser for the umpteenth time, the angry boy silently plots to get even with the world and everyone in it.

≈ *3* ≈

A part of the porch attached to their ample home frames the open, inviting kitchen door while part of it is open to the air and sky. A roof covers half the sturdy, screened-in wooden structure to protect the family from the summer rays. Over the years Annika Williams has gone to great lengths to furnish the screened in area so they can sit outside comfortably and not be "eaten alive," as she says, by the mosquitoes that populate the area in the summertime.

A stately Zebediah Williams stands peacefully meditating on the family's back porch when a wise smile crosses his handsome brown face. At forty he is contented with life's progression. He feels his extremities tingle with happiness brought on by his life with his wife and family. Unaware that Zeb is intensely watching her, Annika digs vigorously in her garden.

Counting silently, Zeb realizes that they've known each other for twenty years now, and he thinks with a gleam in his eyes that at thirty-eight his wife is more lovely than ever. At this moment he understands that Annika's decision made a few years ago was the most difficult of her life. It was then that she gave up the teaching position she loved to stay home to launch their children into adulthood. In spite of that, or maybe because of it, he can see that she's become stronger and more of her own person than he ever anticipated.

As a watchful observer from his position at the rail, he's suddenly overwhelmed with gratitude for the blessings he's received during his life. Memories of their early years flash behind his eyes and Zeb feels awed that their union has been so smooth and problem free over their years of marriage. When they first met, even though it was love at first spark, they both understood those around them would have plenty to say about their pairing.

After all, he thinks, he and his Annika are physically about as opposite as any two people can be. He is a tall, muscular and African-American; Annika is a slim Caucasian woman of medium height with smooth muscles and pale skin. Zeb's family knew that he would always be outgoing and gregarious from the first day he began to talk. In college he was into sports and often ended up in the spotlight because of his athletic and intellectual prowess, a position he never minded. On the other hand, with her quiet nature and contemplative disposition, Annika goes about life never intentionally drawing attention to herself. Her ability to be overlooked easily, a characteristic very unlike Zeb's basic nature, doesn't bother her in the least. Zebediah often thinks that because of their apparent differences it was amazing that he and Annika met at all.

On this afternoon before him Annika crawls about on her hands and knees as she cleans the extensive flowerbeds along their backyard fence. Although totally immersed in the joy of playing in the dirt, as she calls it, Annika knows that even a glimpse of Zeb on the porch still makes her heart race. While her hands work deftly in the soil, her mind wanders to and fro over her life with her husband and children.

Like now, when her heart is flooded with awe for the gifts of love and security she's been given, tears spring to her eyes. As usual, her first reaction is to chide herself for being so soft, so wet. But then Annika decides that's how God made her, for whatever reason. Instead of obsessing over it, she decides to move on, at least for this moment, and concentrates on accepting that characteristic, one she regards as a weakness or flaw in her character.

Annika is suddenly aware of changes in the air and in new scents that bombard her. The heaviness of the air on her skin and the smell of rain in her nostrils overcome the aroma of the glorious dahlias, snapdragons and lavender that surround her. Given a prelude of what's to come in the next moments, Annika digs faster.

When Annika listens, she can hear the gentle ssshhhhhhhh sound rain makes as it's released from the clouds directly above her head. Seconds later, she anticipates and then hears the rapid increase of the first wave of drops. Annika hears the puu, puu, puu sounds as big, fat raindrops hit the ground around her. A split-second later, a bolt of lightning leaps through the sky followed by sharp, insistent claps of thunder. Then, as was anticipated in the afternoon's forecast, the clouds deliver a downpour.

Natural acts, those brimming with power and served up by Mother Nature, have always filled Annika with excitement, and today is no different. Her nerve endings are tweaked by the raindrops and delicious sounds, and send tingles throughout her body. Her first thought is to linger and remain crouched on the ground, protected by her beloved plants and bushes. But soon she decides that isn't such a good idea, so she makes a mad dash for the back porch.

Already the soaking rain plasters her thick hair to her head, and Annika shivers as she sits on the back porch swing, fearful of moving and spreading the soil and rainwater mixture she carried there on her muddy body. She chuckles to herself and suddenly remembers times as a little girl when she found herself covered with mud, loving every moment of it then, too. She muses that there will be some things she'll just never outgrow.

At the first hint of rain Zeb disappears into the house so misses seeing Annika's dash to safety, an action that never fails to entertain him. Within minutes he returns to her carrying a blanket and a steamy mug of hot cider. He quietly hands her the cup, covers her shoulders with the blanket, and slides down on to the glider next to her.

No longer worried about spreading her collection of topsoil and peat, Annika comfortably snuggles into her husband. Zeb wraps his arm around her shoulders and they link their pinky fingers together in a silent vow. During the few storms they've experienced in their life together, Annika remembers that she has always found a peaceful, safe oasis in her husband, with her family and in her home. Reveling in the knowledge that she has always been his anchor as well, they sit smiling and watch the storm pass.

4

They all collect in the kitchen, a homey room filled with family mementos that never fail to bring daily cheer.

An unusual family by some standards, they're all vibrant, bright-eyed and have a desire to squeeze a few words of their own into every lively conversation. The warmth of the daffodil yellow walls and brick red accents embraces each member of the Williams family and calms them during the usual early morning chaos and busy days. Even the dog's wiggle-waggles add her share, too.

At sixteen, Jarren has inherited the best there is to gain from Annika and Zeb's union. The mixture of the genetic inheritance from both his mother and father have left him honey-colored, muscular and an honor student at the local high school. Although naturally intelligent, Jarren prefers school for the socialization with others students, which is more important to him than excelling academically, or even athletically. Recently he's been developing an acute interest in girls, especially smart, athletic ones, but there's no steady girlfriend on the horizon.

At thirteen, Lexi is no shrinking violet and can hold her own in the family and among her peers, too. After several years in the same foster home, one in which Lexi thought she'd remain permanently, her foster mother was suddenly diagnosed with heart problems. The seriousness of the mother's condition required immediate, complex treatment, and prompted Lexi's move to another temporary home under the benevolent supervision of her case worker, Rose Chambers.

Because of the unanticipated changes in Lexi's permanent family plan, she suddenly became available for adoption. Lexi never knew how the whole thing happened, but she was soon told that Reverend Zebediah Williams, his wife and son wanted to enlarge their family by adding her as their second child.

The thirteen-year-old girl believes her social worker must be very persuasive because in no time at all she was meeting Zeb, Annika and Jarren and was soon adopted and placed permanently with the Williams family. The professionals thought that because of Lexi's relatively advanced age and several unsuccessful foster placements, her transition would be more problematic than it has turned out to be.

All along Rose has believed that Lexi was loved dearly as a little girl. Because of that secure first relationship, Lexi has a well-developed ability to love and feel gratitude and is motivated to do well in a family. Consequently, over the past year Lexi's transition into the Williams' home has been amazingly smooth.

As a freshman at the neighborhood Bristol Junior High, Lexi sees herself as a settled in, full member of Annika and Zeb's clan. Maybe due to her intelligence and accepting personality, or a maturity beyond her years, Lexi understands how lucky she is to be adopted by a family as special as this.

Lexi is African-American and has so many traits similar to her parents that often outsiders don't realize that Lexi is not Zeb and Annika's biological child. That assumption doesn't bother anyone in the least. Lexi's best qualities include working hard at her studies and athletic activities, and she never fails to make her parents proud.

On days just like this one, Annika's all-encompassing love for her husband and children spills out through her eyes and flows generously on to everyone in the room. Zeb, dressed in his pastor's garb and ready for the day, reads the morning paper at the table. After their years together, Annika knows that even though he looks involved with the national affairs page, he's completely tuned into Jarren's and Lexi's activities and concerns at the start of each and every day. She loves him even more because he takes the time to keep up with their private worlds and with the big world at large.

Lexi says enthusiastically, "Jarren, show us Lady's new trick."

Happy to show off their dog's skills, Jarren grabs a handful of doggy treats and gestures to the dog. "Okay, girl, you're hurt." Lady lifts her front paw. In mock seriousness, the youth directs the pup, "Now go for help." Lady, a three-year-old mongrel who's obviously part ham, limps dramatically across the kitchen. The family cracks up as the pooch excitedly wolfs down her 'good job' treats.

Even though Annika is laughing and clapping at their cleaver pooch, the mother notices the time and prompts her kids, "You two had better get going or you'll be late for school."

Gently teasing his children, Zeb's slow fake sense of shock reveals the remnants of his Southern upbringing. "Our kids late? Never!"

Pouring on the charm, Jarren sidles up to Annika and tries turning on the charm. "You gonna drive me to school today, Ma, since it's the last day and all?"

Never one for letting things slip by, Lexi asks, "Oh, so now she's your personal chauffeur?"

Jarren retorts, "Don't you know? I'm her favorite son!"

"You're her only son. Dork!" Lexi quips.

Still smiling, Annika reassures them, "Now, now, you're both my favorite, but still no rides to school today."

"Aww, Ma. Please." Jarren pleads.

Like a mother lion, Annika cuffs her son playfully on the arm, "Walking is good for you, Bud. It gives you something to do with all your excess energy."

Both kids collect their books and lunches then kiss Annika on the cheek as they pass her on their way toward the back door. Annika waves goodbye with a shooing motion and a chuckle as they let the door slam behind them.

$\backsim$ **5** $\backsim$

As the kitchen door closes, a look of concentration crosses Annika's face as she makes a mental note of all her plans for the day. She clears the table, pushes the chairs into their resting place, then goes mindlessly into her morning routine.

Preoccupied, Annika doesn't notice that Zeb watches the kitchen door and listens intently for that final click, the one he recognizes as a sign the children are out of the house and on their way to school. As she begins washing dishes, Zeb lightly gets up from the table, and as he approaches Annika from behind, he smiles a sweet sort of devilish smile. Zeb lovingly pats her on the behind and applies sweet, quick kisses to the nape of her neck, but she's intent on getting to the dishes, so doesn't encourage him. Playfully pretending not to notice he's trying to warm her up, Annika enjoys the water on her hands and plays with the bubbles as she submerges the fry pan into the steamy water.

Zeb makes full body contact and whispers dreamily into her ear, "How 'bout some sweet stuff, my sugar?"

Annika giggles and points out what seems so obvious to her, "The kids aren't even out of the yard yet."

Undaunted, Zeb says "So? We're legal, you know."

Sometimes Annika feels torn between her motherly and wifely duties, and as a wave of ambivalence washes over her she says with only a hint of conviction, "Maybe later."

In an effort to convince his bride to join him, Zeb almost whines, "Ah, but sometimes later never comes."

Annika stops what she's doing and looks at him, full face, and remembers why she fell in love with him. She smiles at him and gives him a playful nudge.

Zeb clearly understands Annika's message, however mixed, and laughs a naughty laugh. His voice becomes more throaty, and he persists in snuggling with her in an effort to influence his bride. He says dreamily, "Your mouth says no, but your eyes say..."

He's startled by a noise that takes a few seconds to recognize. Their alone time is suddenly interrupted when Lexi suddenly bursts through the front door. As Lexi crosses the living room heading for the kitchen, she accidentally knocks their most recent family portrait off the side table in her rush. The couple hears the sound of something hitting the floor followed instantly by the tinkling of shattering glass. Since Lexi is bent on completing her task, she's unaware of the mess she leaves behind.

Lexi's noisy entry gives Zeb just enough time to return quickly to a look of innocence behind his newspaper. By the time Lexi reaches the kitchen, her father looks totally involved with the written word before him.

She's excited and doesn't seem to notice what's up with her dad and begins talking before she reaches her mom. She states breathlessly, "Mama, I forgot to get your okay for our field trip today."

"Where are you going?" Annika asks with interest, her mind already diverted from her husband's request.

Enthusiastically, she responds, "To the zoo. The panda had babies and we get to see them!"

As she signs the paper, Annika laughs and says, "Last-Minute-Lexi. Someday, you'll probably be late for your own wedding, Baby."

Lexi smiles a sheepish grin as she gives her mother a quick hug and kisses Zeb on the cheek. She exits the kitchen door, still in a rush.

Over the years Zeb and Annika have figured out that a strong point in their marriage is being able to enjoy the humor of the moment. This is one of those moments. The interruption makes the pair break into gales of laughter. He reaches out for her hand and wordlessly they head up to their bedroom for that sweetness Zeb was looking for earlier.

Before Zeb leaves for his day at the church and Annika gets back to her tasks, they reconnect in a way both of them need, sometimes tenderly and other times desperately.

❦ 6 ❦

While the sun warms her back, Annika is lost in thought as she slowly moves along the flowerbeds in their back yard. Keenly remembering how much she loves summer, she surveys the flowers and notices that the colors are even more brilliant this year. Their beauty is outdone only by the mixture of their intoxicating scents. Big, fat, buzzing bees go about their appointed chores of collecting pollen.

Annika is dressed in sexless work clothes so even Lee, their neighbor from across the back alley, can tell her friend Annika is in her glory. Annika thoughtfully selects certain flowers for cutting and is so engrossed it takes several minutes before she notices Lee waving at her from across the back fence.

Lee nods at the cut flowers laying gracefully in a worn willow basket. "Time to visit Mabel again?" Lee inquires.

Without looking up at her, Annika muses, "Yep, it's my day. I want to take her some of the prettiest I'm got here."

With her usual dose of sarcasm, Lee shares her point of view. "What for? That old biddy is so out of it she doesn't know if you're there or not." Lee adds, "Hell, she wouldn't even know if Tom Selleck flashed her."

Not wanting to match wits with Lee's sarcasm, Annika shrugs and states quietly, "She has no one and it makes me feel good, that's why." Annika squints at Lee, her impatience with her friend's attitude only thinly veiled.

Apparently Lee enjoys her own sassy attitude and continues, "Cut that shit out. Your Mother Teresa approach to life makes the rest of us look bad." Her voice trails off but not before Annika catches the glint in Lee's eyes.

Since she left teaching, Annika has discovered that working in her garden is meditative for her. Every so often, interruptions in her reverie, like this one now, aren't always welcome. Flashing a wry smile, Annika makes a "get outta here" gesture with her hand then turns her attention back to the task at hand.

Suddenly Lady wakes up from her morning nap and darts around the yard while Annika enjoys her pet's abundant energy.

Every once in a while Annika reaches out as if to catch the dog, which only encourages Lady to run and be wilder, a game they both relish to the hilt.

⤚ 7 ⤙

In his minister's garb, Zeb looks stately and almost like African royalty. This morning he surveys his surroundings as he walks through the church making mental notes of what he sees. There's a peace about him that is palpable to those he meets. It takes little imagination, and even strangers can see Zeb has found his calling.

The pastor walks from the church's back door and into the basement area that's been well appointed for social gatherings and large church activities. The Youth and Children's Ministry, one of the distinct joys of his professional life, is in session in an open area. Some adults help the large group of pre-adolescents and teenagers who busily focus on their projects at hand.

Zeb moves from youth to youth, looks over their shoulders at their work, and acknowledges each individual. Zeb knows all the children, their families and life histories, so is aware of how he can help each one when needed. A nudge here and a gentle hand to the shoulder there silently encourages each boy and girl.

The looks of adoration on the children's faces reveal the importance of Zeb's program and how important his attention is in their lives. Many look up from their project to meet his kind, warm eyes, then return to the project. There is no doubt to those who observe the exchanges between the minister and youth that these children know where to come when troubles surface.

Rose Chambers, a middle-aged African-American social worker and friend, who's known Pastor Zeb for a while now, unceremoniously enters the door in the back of the room. Today she has a handsome, sort of angular, blond, light eyed boy in tow. As she moves to Zeb's side, Rose maintains a loose hold on the arm of her wiry charge.

When Zeb sees Mrs. Chambers marching to his side, his face lights up with an infectious warmth. Rose walks the same way as she talks - direct and with purpose. "Good morning, Reverend Williams," she smiles and directs the young boy by gently tugging at his arm. "Carl, say hello to my friend, the Reverend Williams."

Even with the clear instructions Rose provides, Carl appears somewhat uncomfortable. He shuffles his feet and remains silent but nods and then, unexpectedly, he smiles a brilliant smile. Zeb nods and watches their interactions as Rose takes the boy to a seat near the other youngsters.

The social worker gently takes Zeb's arm and pulls him aside, out of hearing distance of the children, and talks to the minister in a quiet voice. It's apparent to Zeb that Rose is being somewhat secretive and he's not sure why.

She shares, "Carl doesn't have a family and has been recently placed on my caseload. I know that Lexi has absolutely blossomed since I placed her with you last year, so I thought of you and Mrs. Williams when we were considering Carl's needs."

With many concerns on his mind, Zeb is distracted by other church matters but soon realizes he just needs to start paying attention to what the social worker is saying. Taken aback by what she's attempting to convey, he takes a deep breath before asking, "What do you know about his history?"

For some reason he thinks Rose is attempting to stifle some of her excitement. The caseworker replies in one of her most non-committal, professional tones, "He's been in foster care for a while, but I think he requires really special parents. This boy has never before had good, loving Christian parents like you and Mrs. Williams before."

Zeb is sometimes quick to recognize wheeling and dealing when he hears it but falls for it this time and can't keep himself from asking more questions. He wonders aloud, "What happened in the other placements? And how many other foster families are you talking about here?"

The minister can see Rose is selecting her words carefully in that trained, mild manner that he's encountered many times before. "Carl can sometimes be sorta headstrong and ran from some homes where the parents were less than sensitive. But," she adds quickly, "he's as smart as a whip and can be so sweet."

Zeb has a few professional moves of his own and intentionally chooses not to show much interest for the moment. He listens intently allowing only traces of concern to reach his usually very expressive face.

When Rose notices the pastor frown ever so slightly, she subtly beefs up her mission and provides him with more information than Zeb may need to make an informed decision.

Rose continues somewhat cautiously, "Kids like Carl, those with disrupted early years, are such strong survivors. Plus that, they certainly come with something extra and will add another dimension to your lovely family." She hesitates for only a nanosecond, then, "I brought Carl over to meet you today because I believe you and Mrs. Williams could provide what he needs."

Zeb thinks for a few moments and then shares his need for caution, "I'll get to know him a little bit today, but I can't promise anything, Rose. I'm sure you know that making major changes in our family dynamics requires a joint decision. I'll need to discuss this with Annika."

Rose nods thoughtfully indicating her understanding of the situation, "All I want is for Carl to have a chance in this world. I think you and Mrs. Williams can offer him the stable, loving life he deserves."

Eyebrows knit, Rose frowns out of concern and anticipation. She needs to leave but lets the boy stay with the group for a while. Zeb watches Carl with keen interest and speaks to him occasionally about nothing in particular. Mostly, however, he just observes the eleven-year-old and sees him interact calmly and easily with the other kids and the adults in charge.

Zeb's internal reaction to his conversation with Rose is one of concern, but so far he's impressed with the young man who seems to be fitting in nicely with his peers.

⇒ *8* ⇐

Zeb has known since shortly after Lexi joined them that Annika is happy and feels fulfilled with their family just as it is now. Mature beyond his years, Jarren adapted well to the addition of new kid sister, Lexi, about a year ago, which has been a relief to all of them. And Zeb often sees Annika smile contentedly during their lively, mostly good–humored exchanges.

Ever sensitive to the needs of his family, Zeb knows that he never wants to pop his wife's happiness bubble or cause his children any unnecessary discomfort. He believes his job as husband and father is to add to the love and peace in their lives. But he still wants to bring the topic up.

Zeb believes he'd never knowingly try to convince Annika to make a decision that would eventually reduce their family serenity. Consequently, he can see that their conversations about Carl have been delicate and fleeting, especially when Annika gives him signals that she isn't in favor of the idea. Even though Carl is an unpopular topic, talks about Carl have progressed at Zeb's urging.

Today the family is spending a day at the park and everyone excitedly prepares for the first picnic of the season. They're all set up at the local park for an afternoon of eating, playing and getting-to-know-Carl fun. Zeb stands at the grill looking very official in his "Chief Chef" apron, while barbecuing chicken and roasting vegetables.

Annika and Lexi chat as they lay out the salads and desserts on a blanket in an attractive arrangement. Jarren keeps the family dog out of the food by keeping her busy with a game of chase the ball, and by the looks of things both boy and dog are having a great time.

Carl was dropped off at the park by his case worker and has just joined them. In an effort to ease any discomfort he may have, Annika wants him to get involved, so hands the boy drinking glasses and asks him to pour lemonade for everyone.

Throughout the afternoon, and even with all the activity, Annika notices that Lady seems to stay close to other kids, and in doing so, avoids Carl. Annika remembers that

Lady was a little shy when they first brought Lexi home. But not to worry, she thinks. The situation with their pet makes sense to her because this is the first time the dog has been around Carl.

In an attempt to welcome Carl and secretly keep peace with her family, Annika smiles at the boy and says warmly, "I'm so glad you came to eat with us, Carl. I sure hope we brought enough food. You look like you could be a good eater."

Carl remains silent, but nods vigorously.

Having experienced similar circum-stances with Lexi, Annika senses how hard this situation might be on Carl and vows to help him feel an accepted part of the family activities. After a few minutes of observation, Annika is curious so decides to be direct and just ask, "I hope you're not afraid of Lady; she's harmless. Do you like dogs?"

Even though she fears she might have pressured him, Carl finally engages and replies, "Yep, I do. And dogs like me too."

The mother thinks his comments don't match her observation and she frowns ever so slightly. Meal preparations are completed so she decides to let it go for now as they sit down on the blanket to eat.

Maybe to make a point, or out of curiosity, Carl reaches out to Lady but rather than coming closer, the pooch ducks nervously behind Lexi. Being closely observant, Annika notices the incident then tucks the information in the back of her mind, determined to think about that later. Other family members seem unaware or don't notice as they begin practically inhaling the smörgåsbord of tasty foods prepared by Annika and Zeb. Besides, the mom muses, this is the first time most of us have met him.

They present a picture to the world of the perfect family. They laugh and joke as they finish their meal. Carl is the only one holding back, but everyone else is having such fun that no one seems to notice.

Still laughing from the jokes and enjoyment of each other's company, Jarren and Lexi prepare to play a card game. In a welcoming gesture to the newcomer Jarren asks, "We're gonna play Uno. Wanna play?"

Lexi enthusiastically chimes in, "We'll teach you if you don't know how to play."

Pleased to be included, Carl nods and moves to the picnic table with Jarren and Lexi. Before sitting down to play, however, the young boy gets another plate and piles it high with food that he grazes on while the three play cards. While the older kids play, Carl listens to the instructions but speaks little.

At peace with the activities of the day Annika and Zeb sit nearby, holding hands and affectionately interacting while they watch the sunset and the children. Lady is tired from her game of fetch so snoozes at Annika's feet.

⤝ *9* ⤞

Annika and Zeb pad around their comfortable bedroom as they prepare for bed, both in the middle of their own bedtime routine. As is usual for her, amid hair brushing and the application of scented creams, Annika quietly muses over the activities of her day. During adolescence she discovered that contemplative exercises like reviewing her day seems to help her gain new perspectives on life events. It also helps her "puts things in order," as she calls those quiet meditative times.

Zeb's ending routine usually involves reading new self-help books and a few verses from his Bible. However, as is consistent with his personality, often Zeb wants to talk. Although loathe to interrupt her peace, Zeb knows the topic he wants to bring up and, if he doesn't do it tonight, fears the opportunity for the discussion may pass.

So he takes a deep breath and goes for it, "What do you think about Carl, Annika?"

"He's polite enough," she replies, "but don't you think he's sorta like a little old man? I think he seems way older than eleven in some ways." She hesitates then adds, "And did you see how much food he put away in that little frame of his?"

Zeb had noticed as well and was equally amazed and states, "Yes. It's like he thought he would never get another meal. Ever!"

They both sigh as they recall the sight of the small boy, eating constantly from plates of food piled high before him.

Annika continues, "I'm sure glad to see the kids made him feel welcome. Jarren was nice like that to Lexi when we adopted her, too. Do you remember that?"

She nods while he thoughtfully summons the courage to broach a new aspect of the topic. Cautiously, Zeb asks, "Do you think if Carl were to join our family it would go as well as it has with Lexi?"

Her eyes open wide as she looks directly at him in total surprise. Annika is unable to mask her shock, and asks, "Are you really thinking of adopting another child?"

Zeb suspects he might be on thin ice. He also believes intuitively that he and Annika will be at opposite ends of the pole over the idea of adopting another child. Fearful his courage will disappear, he quickly responds, "Uh-huh. Don't you remember how we always dreamed about having a few kids and then adopting more?"

Maintaining a direct gaze at her husband, Annika nods indicating her memory of those old conversations but doesn't rush to respond. After what seems to Zeb like minutes of silence, she speaks, "Yes, but that was a while ago, when I was younger. Time has passed since then." With an unexpected spurt of energy she goes on, "I don't think I can give another child what he needs and have time for the rest of you, too."

Sounding very much like the pastor he is and aware of his need to tread lightly, Zeb nearly purrs, "Aww, Baby, God has blessed you with a lion's share of patience and love."

Her mates' slightly off-handed gestures communicates a message to her that he's not worried about the issue or about how many inner resources Annika has or doesn't have. She's beginning to feel pressured and is slightly irritated by it.

"I'm not sure I agree with your assessment of what God's gifts are or have been for me," she replies, starting to sound almost testy. "And what about my energy level? I no longer have unlimited energy to give to everyone and anyone around me who needs something," Annika states thoughtfully.

Although he's not worried about what she lacks, at first he remains silent and then lovingly interrupts the discussion with an enveloping embrace and places gentle kisses all over her sleep-prepared face.

Zeb doesn't intend to increase her fears but unknowingly dismisses them out of his enthusiasm to do God's work, as he often describes his enthusiastic approach to settling dilemmas. When he feels Annika relax in his arms, he whispers, "We have room for Carl." Then, after some moments of hesitation, he speaks softly, "I'd like to call Rose tomorrow. Okay?"

The lines between her brows deepen ever so slightly. He's so into his own thoughts and the gesture so minute that Zeb completely misses the worry on her face or in her voice.

Annika has known for her entire married life that pleasing Zeb and making sure he's happy is her job and one of her marital missions. Often their compromises turn out with both of them getting their needs met and feeling okay about which path to take.

Usually, Annika doesn't feel like she's being pressured to agree with him. This time, however, she reacts with a slow nod, the kind that's fraught with more meaning than can be spoken in the moment.

Along with a nearly audible buzz of energy, there's a slightly perceptible tension filling the air. The Williams family is bustling and everyone has a part to play in today's drama. The room is bright, cheerful and decorated in athletic décor, like a Home & Gardens room that's been designed just so for a young boy. And that's especially true for this eleven-year-old boy.

They're excited and everyone is happy to have a part in getting ready for Carl to join their family. During the preparation they all entertain their own secret versions of what it will be like having a new family member.

Annika tidily makes Carl's bed and covers it with a new red, white and blue bedspread and fluffy throw pillows. Jarren thoughtfully rearranges decorative items on the dresser again and again until it looks just right to him. Lexi waters a leafy, live plant with a "Welcome" balloon attached to a stick, then puts it on the nightstand next to his bed. Zeb gently places a pen and paper on the new desk and puts them in the best light. After the preparations are completed he stands at the door overlooking his family with enormous pride and a huge grin across his face.

Suddenly the doorbell rings louder than they've ever heard it and everyone jumps with a start. They collectively scurry downstairs to the front door and Zeb, in his excitement, gets there first.

As the door is opened, Carl is there with shiny eyes and an excited look on his scrubbed face. He stands in the entry just slightly in front of Rose and looks a little nervous. His jeans and t-shirt look new but it's impossible for Zeb and Annika to tell that the trash bag he carries holds the rest of his personal items. He clutches the bag very tightly.

Zeb glows, steps aside gesturing them into the room, and says just a little too loudly, "Welcome to our family, Son."

Wanting to echo her husband's sentiments, Annika instinctively knows the boy isn't ready for a hug, as she always greets Jarren and Lexi. Instead, she welcomes Carl by putting her hand on his shoulder and patting him. He immediately pulls away from her in a move too subtle for the others to notice and maintains a distance from her. Annika is puzzled by his gesture and makes a mental note of it.

In one cohesive group they move through the house showing him around, and they finally arrive at his bedroom. Carl's eyes widen as he enters the room and examines everything closely. Slowly he moves around the room as his fingertips explore all that his eyes can see. They watch him with wonder as Carl's vision bathes every item, every nook and cranny, everything that's there for the seeing.

Zeb and the other children behold the moment with awe and after several minutes decide to go into the hall beyond his door to give Annika and Carl a few minutes together. Zeb believes the first few moments of his new life with them is special, almost sacrosanct, and is to be acknowledged with reverence.

Annika looks calm on the outside but internally is amazed to discover that she feels so much excitement and is almost gushy about this moment, and about this child. She is somewhat surprised by her inner response but has learned over the last few years that among her better qualities, she is at her best when just being a mom. Any reluctance she's experienced over the last few days dissipates during this exhilarating event.

Feeling a wave of warmth ripple over her, Annika leans toward the boy and says, "I'm so glad you're here, Carl. We're very happy to have you as part of our family." So as not to overwhelm him, she waits a minute and says, "We've had fun fixing your room up for you. I hope you like it."

Carl offers very little in response, so she keeps trying, "Wow, first day! Is there anything you need to know?"

Maintaining some of the distance he'd exhibited in the first minutes, he looks at her with some suspicion in his old eyes and asks, "What should I call you?"

Annika responds thoughtfully, "Mom and Dad works for us, but, don't worry, Sweetheart, you'll get the hang of it here."

"Yeah, I guess," he says with no detectable enthusiasm.

Still full of excitement and wanting to celebrate Carl's arrival, Annika picks this moment to walk to the closet and open the door. The experienced mother has an idea what to do in the circumstance and brings a huge stuffed polar bear out of the closet and places it softly on the bed near him. "For you," she says choked up with emotions.

Carl looks at her with totally blank eyes.

Annika's nerves suddenly jangle and she finds herself talking too much, sort of like she's trying to convince him of something. Unable to stop herself, she chatters on, "We want you to be part of our family." She wants him to know that being a full member of their family is his for the taking, with all the joys and responsibilities.

And then she presses too hard, "I'd like you to be with us in our activities. We play together and do chores together, too. Please take care of your room and make your bed every day, just like the other kids do."

For some reason unknown to her, Carl selects that exact instant to turn so only she can see his expression. She is stunned when he flashes her a cold, intimidating look that sends shivers all the way down her spine. Carl's murderous glare was fleeting but impresses Annika in a negative way.

Then, just as suddenly, he turns in the direction of the others still waiting in the hall outside his door and smiles a broad, toothy grin at them. Carl then walks out of the bedroom and joins the rest of his new family. They are delighted.

The anxious mother suddenly feels like a statue that's been struck by a bolt of lightning. Electrified and unable to move, she thinks that she's never met such a child or had an experience like that ever before. Annika also wonders what it all means, if anything.

⮶ *11* ⮴

You get to it through a door off the second floor hall. Unless someone introduces you to it or shows you the way to the attic, the door is indistinguishable from the closets or other doors to rooms that line the long front-to-back hall.

Once inside the stairwell to the third floor are shallow and narrow, perhaps it was a path built in the early 1900's for small people with tiny feet. The top level used to be full of boxes and hand-me-downs, but nowadays it's been converted into a charming, comfortable place to go to dream dreams and capture some of the wonder left over from days gone by.

As Zeb and Carl reach the third floor attic, the air feels hotter and thinner than even one floor below. Carl is thoughtful as the pair wanders through the room at the top of the Williams' home. Suddenly Carl's eyes widen in astonishment, and he can't believe what his eyes behold.

In the center of the broad room sits an elaborate Lionel train set. It's one like few have ever seen, one that covers a huge, makeshift table top that balances on four, paint-splattered saw-horses. The tracks carry the intricately painted train over hills and dale, around boulders and through miniature evergreen woods. Small buildings hold make believe woodsmen and model train depots provide shelter for imaginary citizens.

As he examines the set, Zeb gets lost in memories of happy days during his southern childhood. The father smiles a knowing smile and gently rearranges the scenery on the table as he did so long ago. Carl quietly ponders the scene before him.

After many silent minutes, Zeb pulls himself back to the present and says with a voice full of emotion, "This is the train set my father gave me. We worked on it for hours when I was your age."

Instantly Carl looks terrified but remains silent and into himself. Zeb looks quizzically at the boy but doesn't comment on the change. He decides to save the observation until later and continues playing with the pieces he treasures.

Wanting to help Carl become part of their family, Zeb continues, "You can play with this if you would like. Do you like trains?"

Carl nods dumbly and looks anxious for no reason Zeb can grasp, but keeps his distance from the train and the table.

Zeb goes on, "Since this train set is so big and sorta complicated to operate, please ask Jarren or me for help for a while. Okay?"

Carl nods again but is unable to hide a strange, distracted look from his face, one that Zeb can't possibly understand.

☞ *12* ☜

It's dark outside as Carl lies in his bed reading by the light of his boyish bedside lamp that looks like a baseball bat and glove. While he reads, his expressions fluctuate from disbelief, to relief, and then to angry tension.

As Annika knocks and enters Carl's room, she experiences an internal shudder as she sees the title of Carl's book, "Tales From the Grave." Without any objections from him, she pulls the shades down and then slowly sits on the edge of his bed. This has become a usual part of his bedtime routine, a time for mother and son to review their day and say goodnight.

As gently as possible, Annika removes the book from his hands and says softly, "Time for bed, Sweetheart," and in spite of her efforts to avoid a reaction from Carl, he immediately looks distressed and tries to grab the book away from her. Her internal good mom thinks that her actions may have been a little too abrupt so she tries to soften them by placing his treasured book on his bedside stand next to the dead plant and limp 'Welcome' balloon.

Annika lovingly pulls his covers up to his chin and tucks him in. "Good book?" she inquires fighting to remain neutral toward the book with such a horrendous title.

Carl states defensively and more clearly than she's ever heard him speak before, "My mom gave it to me."

Annika is surprised at the mention of his mother and works to maintain a calm exterior. She wants to use the time to get to know him better so adds, "Then it must be very special to you."

She's learned recently that when he has no eye contact or makes no attempt to open up or respond to Annika's invitations to chat, the message she gets is to leave the topic alone. She gingerly decides to change direction and asks with warmth in her voice, "So how do you like being here, Carl?"

The boy shrugs but it's apparent that he has something else, something big on his mind. Annika watches him take time to screw up his courage, Carl takes the risk and asks, "When can I do the same things the other kids do?"

Surprised, yet pleased by his unexpected gumption, Annika leans toward him and replies, "You'll eventually get to do more, Honey. But you're younger, so it may never seem quite fair." She pauses and wonders, "Do you have anything special on your mind?"

Carl returns to his surly attitude and says, "Nah, not really."

So far, the mother knows instinctively that there are times to remain vague and other times when it's okay to encourage him to talk to her, so Annika adds, "Let me know if you do."

Nonchalantly, Carl replies, "Yeah, whatever."

Feeling like they were getting somewhere, Annika gets up from the bed and states enthusiastically, "Good. Time to sleep, Darling. I'll tuck you in."

Carl's face goes stormy as his head fills with the faint sound of a train chugging by in the distance.

Sometimes she can see that he appears engrossed in some other time, some other place, but decides to prepare him for bed anyway. Annika lightly tugs at Carl's covers as she leans in to kiss him on the cheek. Without warning, Carl suddenly brings his knees sharply up to his chest and from the fetal position slams his head into Annika's nose.

The excruciating moment brings a look of horror to Annika's face and tears to her eyes. She gasps in pain as she jumps away from his bedside. Her hands fly to her face and clutch her nose in an attempt to stop blood from gushing through her fingers. Annika cries with the sound of a wounded animal.

Carl's face changes immediately, barely hiding a hint of pleasure from Annika's pain. Sounding somewhat unconvincing while looking more collected than his mother, he says, "Oh, sorry, Mommy. I did that on accident. Sorry!"

Then Carl quickly switches off the bedside lamp and rolls over to face the sports posters hanging on his wall by the bed. Annika stands stunned in the darkness, unable to determine what needs to be done first and confused by the sudden personality change she'd just seen in her youngest son.

By the time Annika rushes to their bathroom down the hall, her face, hands and arms are covered with warm, sticky blood. She leans over the sink and tries to clean herself up as Zeb wanders by the open door of the bathroom and sees her.

Zeb nearly shouts with terror in his voice, "Annika!"

He lovingly sits her down on the toilet, grabs a towel and begins blotting her face. Even though Annika always hates to cry, she weeps like a baby and cannot seem to make herself quit. It seems like an eternity to her before she is able to catch her breath or speak.

"It was just an accident," Annika weakly assures her husband. "My nose hit Carl's head when I kissed him goodnight." Between her remaining tears she can see that Zeb is still filled with horror, so adds, "Don't worry, I'm a mess, but I'm all right."

As his face crinkles up with concern for his wife's distress, Zeb states lovingly, "You don't look all right. Are you sure?"

Simultaneously trying to convince her husband and to console herself, Annika shares, "I'm okay. Really! It just surprised me, that's all. He didn't mean to hurt me."

Annika is at a place where she can snuggle with him a bit, and does. "Please, Babe," she murmurs into his chest, "don't give it another thought."

⤝ 13 ⤜

The flowers and bushes in the Williams' backyard are in full bloom thanks to the TLC given by Annika. At some point the shrubs are trimmed neatly but she encourages the spirea and hibiscus plants to grow naturally wild and free. Tulips and iris of many colors adorn fertile flowerbeds and surround an area of deep green grasses left that way so the family has a place to play catch and throw frisbee.

Carl surreptitiously skirts the backyard looking under and between the trees and bushes. His behaviors might not make sense to onlookers, but it's apparent that every one of his movements makes sense to him.

Lady spends a lot of time outside in the fenced back yard during the mild weather, an activity that she enjoys. But today, when Carl is here, Lady dashes there. When the boy runs toward the dog, Lady cowers and hides in the dark undergrowth near an old building way back in the yard.

Tired of the unsuccessful game of catch-the-dog, Carl sits on the bottom porch step but still tries to entice the pooch into playing the game. Carl calls the dog repeatedly, but with a mind of her own, she doesn't cooperate or give in to the boy's demands. Lady becomes increasingly anxious and barks uncontrollably at him before she dashes off again to hide.

Eventually frustrated with her unco-operative responses, Carl hisses in voice so low that no one except Lady can hear him, "Fucking bitch of a dog!" Then, when Lady still doesn't come to him, Carl stomps up the steps and slams his way into the house.

⤜ *14* ⤛

Annika sits in the comfy living room chair, enjoying the temporary peace and quiet of their home.

The silence is suddenly broken as Carl enters, baseball glove, bat and ball in hand. Before he acknowledges his mother's presence, he dramatically flops on the couch with a look of total disgust across his face.

Annika happily acknowledges his presence but decides not to address the body slam he's just delivered to the sofa.

"Hi, Honey," she says with as much warmth as she can muster. "How was practice?"

Carl shrugs and complains with a growl, "I don't like Coach. He always lets others play more than me." On a roll now he adds, "I pitched good, but he still made me play outfield and put some jerk in my place."

Working at remaining calm and sounding positive, Annika replies, "Ah, that's too bad. But, you know Carl, there's nothing wrong with playing outfield. Somebody's gotta play there."

Collecting steam, Carl goes on, "I don't wanna play outfield. I should pitch! I'm the best player they've got on the team and those other punks are totally lame."

Suddenly feeling defensive and not happy about it, she adds, "That can't be true. Everybody who plays tried out for the team, just like you did." She tries to reason with the complaining boy before her. "Why don't you like them?"

Carl doesn't respond to her toned down approach by becoming calmer. Instead, he continues to whine, "They don't know how to play and Coach likes them better than me."

Still trying to be the voice of reason and turn this into a teachable moment, Annika remarks, "Is there any possibility you're being a little oversensitive, Honey?"

Incensed that Annika is blaming this on him, he screams, "Fuck you, Annika! You don't know shit. You're just a girl."

With more steam than usual, Carl wings his glove and ball across the room and slams his bat on the floor. He begins lurching himself around the room giving no thought to the wisdom of his reaction or the kicks to the coffee table. Magazines scatter, and when the glass clock and vase hit the floor with such force, they shatter into hundreds of pieces.

With his fists closed tightly and the muscles of his clenched jaw standing out, Carl is not yet finished and makes a statement by wiping his muddy shoes on the couch. In a split second he jumps in front of Annika and intentionally looms over her. It takes every fiber of her being to remain in her chair and not react out of the anger or frustration she's feeling. She's afraid that any sudden reactions from her will aggravate the situation so she sits as perfectly still as she can.

He glares threateningly into Annika's eyes with a stone cold 'just try to stop me' look. Then, without a word or explanation, Carl charges out of her face and leaves the room. Annika sits frozen in her seat trying to understand what just happened. She also decides she needs to sit long enough for her racing heartbeats to subside. After time enough for her adrenaline level to return to normal she gets up slowly and sadly begins cleaning up his mess.

Annika thinks that if her family had been present at that exact moment and had seen Carl's behavior, they would know for sure that he has a problem. But never having experienced Carl in a similar situation, she is sad to think they may never actually see the truth.

~

At the end of his work day Zeb enters through the kitchen door. She sees in an instant that he looks at her with eyes that secretly wish she would run to him with open arms. Instead, Annika stands quietly at the stove stirring dinner.

Zeb is chatty and shares details of his day. He thinks his bride, as he often refers to her, looks upset so he makes it a point to give her an 'I'm glad to see you' kiss and uses the, "Hi, Anni. How's your day?" approach.

Although she's not usually sarcastic, Annika musters some up. Her 'My day was just fine' comment has the kind of tone Zeb is never eager to hear.

At that moment Carl walks into the kitchen and searches the refrigerator for something to eat. Just out of the shower with his hair all slicked down, he nearly sparkles. Annika notices that he avoids eye contact with her, as usual she thinks, but grins large and looks directly into Zeb's eyes and nearly coos, "Hi, Daddy!"

Zeb responds in kind, "Hey, Buddy. How did practice go?"

The youth nearly bubbles. "Great! Coach let me pitch," the boy brags. "I get to start the next game."

"That's my boy!" purrs the proud dad.

Annika remains silent but watches their exchange in total disbelief.

～

Later that night, Annika turns down the bed then sits at her dressing table to brush her hair. After a few minutes, instead of bursting out loud as she would have preferred to relieve lots of pent-up emotions, she begins to cry quietly.

Zeb is sitting in his comfy chair nearby catching up on his reading when he tunes into what she's doing and becomes confused. Genuinely concerned, Zeb asks, "What's up, Sweetheart?"

Collecting herself, Annika finishes her internal argument and finds herself ready to share only a bit with her husband. She responds heavily, "I'm worried."

"Worried about what?" Zeb wonders aloud.

He sees she is pensive and full of emotion, a situation that is something he's rarely seen with her. Annika considers what all she could say but selects only a few words in hopes of bringing Zeb into her world.

She begins slowly, "I don't think I'm doing so well with Carl." She hesitates again, then adds, "We were talking today about playing baseball and the team and he suddenly became completely unglued."

He's learned through their years of marriage that under such serious times he must remain silent and be fully attentive to give her the time she needs to sort her thoughts.

Measuring her words, she continues carefully, "But he sure lights up when you come home."

Not waiting any longer, he attempts to console Annika with sympathy. "Ah, Babe, he's still adjusting. You know this won't be easy on either of you. In fact, I think the adjustment will be harder on you two than on the rest of us."

Although that sounds reasonable to Annika, especially with the bonding that is necessary between between a mother and her child, she's still unconvinced. "Why do you say that?" she asks.

Zeb takes a deep breath, checks his thoughts to make sure they're accurate, then adds, "You want to make him happy and he wants to please you. He just hasn't been here long enough to learn the ropes yet."

Hoping against hope, Annika replies, "I suppose you're right. It's true, I'd love to make the process move faster than it is." She concedes, "I guess I'm just tired."

Out of his love and desire to support his wife, and pleased they're on the same page, Zeb states, "Yeah, it's still too early to be worried. Hang in there, Honey. It'll turn out just right." And almost as an afterthought, he adds, "I promise."

Annika wants her husband to be right. Her thoughts are disturbing to her but she doesn't want to dampen Zeb's excitement about making this family the one of his dreams. When they climb into bed, Zeb, in true form, cradles and kisses his soul mate then falls asleep smiling.

Wrapped deep in his strong, brown arms, Annika still worries.

⌐ *15* ⌐

It's a beautiful spring day at the town ballpark. Even the cheerfully chirping birds seem to sense the excitement in the air. With perfectly appointed grounds the lines around the field are stark in their newness. In contrast, the old whitewashed, wooden bleachers show the sitzmarks and footprints of fans from seasons past.

There in the center, in the spot they believe gives them the best view, the entire Williams family snuggles together happily rooting for their newest member.

On Coach Tomes' cue, Carl moves from the dugout to the field with his teammates. Annika identifies Carl from among his teammates as they leave the dugout and head onto the field. Many of the boys run smiling to their assigned positions, chattering as they go.

Carl is distinctive with his sullen look as he places himself shallow in right field and stubbornly stands his ground. Coach also observes Carl's lack of enthusiasm and motions him to move deeper into the field, but Carl pretends not to understand. He stands wooden at the spot he selects.

After three outs with no plays they return to the dugout. Carl is sullen and sits alone at the end of the bench. The other boys stand at the fence cheering their team on, just as they've been taught. When his teammates call for him to join them, he just glares at them and stays glued to his seat.

Always trying to understand her brood, Annika finds Carl's eye contact, or lack of it, interesting. She sees that Carl makes fleeting eye contact with Jarren and Lexi and throws dirty looks frequently at his coach between plays and when he's on the field. Annika also thinks he glares at his teammates when they talk to him. Perhaps her son is something of a bluffer, Annika thinks, and, in spite of what he says, maybe he really does like the coach and the other boys.

But what Annika notices mostly, which is amazing to her, is that Carl often looks directly at Zeb with looks that seemed to beg for his approval. The most interesting to her of all, however, is his lack of eye contact with her. He seems to avoid her completely. In response to her observation, Annika silently chides herself about a newfound paranoia that's developed since Carl joined their family. Why she thinks that she's not sure, but then she reminds herself to think less and watch the game more.

Her intense scrutiny is sharply interrupted by the gruff bark of the umpire, Larry. "Batter up!"

Happy that it's finally his turn at bat, Carl steps up to the plate. The boy looks determined to hit the ball into next week, as he often wishes and have it be the one that wins their game.

Up in the press box, behind all the fans, the announcer sits at the microphone. Unkempt and sweaty, Troy is known for really getting into the game and it's been that way since he played ball in high school over ten years ago.

He nearly shouts into the microphone, "It's the bottom of the ninth, with two outs, and two on base. We've got a 4-2 ball game here. Williams, at bat, is hoping to close the gap and finish up this game with a win for the home team!"

In spite of a desire to do otherwise, Carl looks very nervous. They can see his knuckles are white and he's clenching his jaw from their seat on the bleachers. They can see his lips move as he tries to rattle the pitcher on the mound, but can't hear him as he hisses under his breath, "No pitcher here."

The family cheers gleefully as Carl steps up to the plate. Annika, Zeb, and their kids wildly call to him with the usual instructions parents give when their kids are at bat. "Atta boy!" they shout. "Keep both eyes on the ball!" and "It only takes one!"

Carl sizes up the first pitch too late and lets it go by. He's pissed. When he swings and misses the second pitch, his face becomes contorted and turns crimson. Carl's anger rapidly becomes obvious to those watching the game. While the boy prepares for the next pitch, his attention is interrupted by the sounds of distant trains chugging through his head.

He fights to return to the moment as he growls at the ump, "Get some glasses! You're blind!"

Carl just can't quit. He adjusts his stance and glares his most intimidating stare, then screams sarcastically at the pitcher, "Hey, Girly, gimme something I can hit!"

Wound like a tight coil, Carl holds the bat high and behind his head. He swings violently at the final pitch, but misses it and knocks himself off balance with the movement. As he recovers his footing, he slings his bat with all his might toward his own dugout, charges the mound, cursing as he runs full throttle.

Coach Tomes, with his reputation for being gruff but always fair, moves fast and intercepts Carl before he reaches the mound. The boy, extraordinarily strong for his age, is filled with adrenaline, and a physical struggle ensues.

In an effort to get him under control, Coach pins him to the ground and restrains him, shouting, "Carl, get a grip!"

Carl can't control himself and snarles at Coach through clenched teeth. "We woulda' won if you knew what the fuck you're doing."

The coach looks angry, then perplexed, but doesn't want to engage in an argument with the boy. Instead he hollers, "Four laps around the field for that language. Now!"

Reluctantly, Carl climbs out of the dirt and runs to the perimeter of field. He is still so angry that he grumbles in the coach's direction as he runs, "I'm the best player on this team and you stick me in the fucking outfield."

After the final lap Carl comes to a screeching stop in front of Coach and struggles to catch his breath. He still has some attitude left and states angrily, "It's not my fault we lost."

Heads bowed in embarrassment, Jarren and Lexi walk quickly off the field and return to their car. Annika and Zeb are incredulous and stunned that their youngest son had to be restrained over what looked like a minor infraction. More shocked than Annika, Zeb is especially puzzled by Carl's outburst.

As Zeb and Annika reach the pair, they hear the Coach's instructions. "That's right, Carl, it's nobody's fault." Fighting to keep himself under control, he adds, "Always, always, one team wins and the other team loses. That's baseball!" Tomes concludes, "During the next game I expect you to mind yourself, young man."

Zeb gives Coach Tomes a few minutes to catch his breath. With a serious frown on his handsome face and trying to take the whole scene in, Zeb reaches out to shake the coach's hand. "Thanks for working with him, Coach. Wow, he's got some hot temper there."

In a respectful hushed voice, Mr. Tomes shared, "Lately I've noticed that Carl has a problem getting along with the other players, too. He doesn't try to fit in with them and stays off by himself most of the time." With some hesitancy Coach adds, "I think he'll come around with some guidance though. We'll keep at it and see if we can turn him around."

Speaking on the couple's behalf, Zeb stated, "My wife and I appreciate your efforts with him, Coach. Carl is a strong-willed boy, but real bright. I think he'll catch on fast."

As the parents thank Coach Tomes, they nod to Carl, a sign that it's time to head home. As they cross the field toward their waiting car, Annika reaches out in a motherly way to put her hand on Carl's shoulder. Annika is taken by surprise when, like before, the youth roughly shrugs away from her touch, and reacts inwardly. Then, with a quick change of position, but before she has time to respond, Carl somehow steps on the instep of her foot with his full weight.

Annika flinches in pain and wipes away the tears that spring to her eyes. She again wonders about what message her son is trying to give her.

⁓ *16* ⁓

It's early evening, Annika's favorite time of day. She is always excited about this time of day because she knows that soon her family will return from their daily activities, full of chatter about their time out in the world. She loves to watch their faces animated with emotion while they tell their stories.

The afternoon sun leaves a dappled pattern on the kitchen counter while a playful breeze rushes through the bushes below the window providing sounds and fragrances that tantalize her senses. While she waits, she slowly mixes the ingredients to an old family favorite, a dish that always brings back memories of dinners past, and smiles.

Annika hears her children playing at a distance, a note that all is well. She remembers times when those sounds consoled her soul, but that's not been the case recently.

While Annika reminisces, she attempts to trim the excess fat off the meat and looks in another drawer for a particular knife she always uses for that task. During the initial search she finds nothing so she becomes unexpectedly more frantic as she dives deeper into the drawers where their special knives are kept.

She looks further and cannot find what she seeks. "Hmmm? Where's that old knife?" she says softly under her breath. Annika frowns and is puzzled.

Her intense search is suddenly inter- rupted by a loud cry from the sounds of a wounded animal in their backyard. As Annika rushes to look out the kitchen window, she hears Lady cry again and then she sees her dog running away from Carl.

Curious about the interchange between their beloved pet and Carl, she quietly observes a bit longer. Now even more confused, Annika sees her son squatting near the back fence holding a cord in his hand. He gives Lady a hateful stare as he mouths silent words to the dog who keeps her distance.

Annika can't tell what is going on, but she thinks the situation looks bad.

~

The early evening is pleasant with the warm light of twilight combined with a lazy breeze, a perfect time for a walk. After the dinner dishes are dried and put away, Annika collects Lexi and Carl for a walk through the neighborhood. They start out the front door when Annika remembers something. She turns around and goes back into the house but soon returns with a very worried look on her face.

She frowns and says, "I can't find Lady."

Lexi is tuned into her mother and looks worried as well. The girl shakes her head making a silent statement that she doesn't know where Lady could be either.

Carl looks unusually calm which makes Annika wonder. "Carl," Annika tries to sound more casual than she feels, and asks, "Do you have any idea where she might be?"

He calmly replies clearly, "No, Annika, I don't."

She cautiously presses the issue, "When did you last see her?"

Looking directly into her eyes, which Annika finds unusual but interesting, Carl comments plaintively, "I played with her this morning and heard her bark a while ago. Didn't you hear her, Mommy?"

Annika and Lexi shake their heads in unison while Annika tries to mask her growing fears. "Let's look for her while we're out," the mother suggested calmly. "She probably just got out of the yard. Or, maybe she has a boyfriend around the block."

❧ *17* ❦

The Williams' house sits on a lush two-acre lot. A quarter of the back yard they refer to as "the garden" is where Annika spends much of her energy pulling and plucking and making the view beautiful. Because of that, the fenced-in garden is manicured and full of well-tended, colorful flowers of many colors and a wide variety of easily managed bushes.

Behind that section is the back lot which is a completely different story. Left pretty much in its natural state, the area is filled with grasses, saplings and several mature trees. Their mini-forest acts as a buffer zone and provides them with privacy that's hard to find in their neighborhood.

Half hidden in that area is a wooden, low-slung building that sits in the farthest corner of the back lot. Used for storage and as an extra garage, it's nearly hidden by a winter's worth of firewood that's stacked against the back wall.

As dusk approaches, Annika is sick with worry about Lady. Against her natural instincts she waited for her pet to return home on her own, but so far that hasn't happened. In spite of Zeb's encouragement she's unable to make herself wait one more minute. Now there is no other choice, she just has to find Lady.

Early this morning she combed the neighborhood and alerted her neighbors to be on the look out for the dog. Annika feels more frustrated than ever and decides she needs to look closer to home. Searching the garden, Annika becomes more frantic, and as she enters the back lot through a rusty, mostly unused gate, she feels the anxiety rise sharply into her chest.

Annika's expression turns to terror as she begins shouting, "Lady! Lady, where are you?" Annika whistles for the dog as she looks up to the sky and pleads with God, "I know Lady's just a dog, but she is important to me." She pauses then adds, "Please, God, please let her be okay."

Tears trickle down her face as she carefully winds her way through the lot as she examines every nook and cranny, every mound of grass and behind every stick of wood. The anxious mom finds nothing unusual, which is a relief to her, but she's having difficulty convincing her pounding heart.

Suddenly, Annika stops short with sheer alarm written on her face. With eyebrows knit she leans toward the ground and looks intently at a pile of dirt she finds behind the shed. First she pokes at it with a stick she finds nearby, but immediately tosses the branch aside, drops to the her knees and furiously brushes the soil from atop the mound.

Annika bursts into sobbing spasms and calls out to her Maker, "Oh my God! Oh, God. Lady, what happened?"

Still kneeling on the ground and with trembling hands, Annika slowly brushes the loose soil off Lady's body. When Lady is freed from her shallow grave, she pulls the body of the lifeless dog onto her lap. Annika is horrified to see her pet has been slit from her throat, through the belly, all the way to her tail with her innards spilling out on the ground. Lady's muzzle is tied tightly with a cord.

Annika sits for what seems like hours holding her dear Lady, unable to do anything but sob. After many minutes she collects her courage and what is left of her pet, stands up and begins to head toward the house.

Eventually Annika comes to and reconsiders her plan. Instead, she reverently lays Lady down, walks slowly to the shed to get a shovel, and then carefully selects a spot nearby. In one of the most difficult acts in her life, Annika methodically digs a hole then places her pet in the grave for all time.

Once Lady is buried to her liking, Annika covers the site with leaves to make the sacred site look indistinguishable from any other. She says a silent prayer, then returns the shovel to its place in the shed.

Bereft, Annika tries to make sense of all this, but can't. It's too bizarre for her to comprehend. She musters all her strength as she walks slowly across the lot, into the garden, and toward the kitchen door. On this, the darkest day in her life, Annika drags herself through the door fighting to gain control of her emotions.

Heartbroken, she is unsure how she will ever deliver such bad news to her family.

⤙ *18* ⤚

Annika knows that trips to the local grocery can be challenging even on the best days, but that's especially true when she's in a rush. Today it's nearly supper time and Carl and Annika are both tired and at their crankiest. Just inside the front door Annika sees that the grocery store is in bedlam and full of mothers with hungry, demanding children of all ages.

Maybe this wasn't such a good idea, she thinks. Nonetheless, against all odds Annika is determined to get in and out quickly. She whips the cart down the aisles while Carl lags behind, sulking every inch of the way.

Feeling totally frustrated, she half yells trying to get through to him, "What do you want for breakfast?"

Carl responds with no enthusiasm, "Dunno."

With all her might she tries to get cheerful so she can get through to him in a pleasant way. Most of all, Annika doesn't want to catch any more of the free-floating anxiety that seems to be hovering in the air throughout the market. With lips that are only slightly pursed she states, "I don't mean now, Honey. What do you want me to buy for you for later?"

It looks to her that Carl's dragging of his feet is intentional. And ignoring her is, too. Appearing to be uninterested in much of anything, and maybe to communicate his unhappiness at being at the market, the boy swats at the products lining the shelves.

Annika is certain that he's also disinterested in being with her. As hard as she tries, Annika isn't able to help herself and adds to the tension by getting testy. She quips sarcastically, "Simple question, Carl. This job will be easier if I don't have to guess what you want to eat."

He persists in swinging his arms in the air and finally Carl knocks down a food display at the end of the counter adding to the general bedlam in a major way. As he jumps back from the flying boxes, she sees him break out in a sly little smile.

"Carl!" Annika nearly shouts with a corrective tone that's out of character for her.

Still surly and attempting to portray himself as innocent, the boy replies, "Wh-a-t?"

He hasn't caught on to her instructions yet, so Annika's voice gets tighter and higher pitched the longer she explains. "I don't want to fight with you," she states emphatically. Still trying to reason with the stubborn youth, she pleads, "If we help each other we'll be out of here in no time and this could even be pleasant. Now pick those boxes up."

Carl simply glares at Annika letting her know with a flash of his great eyes that he doesn't buy her logic and isn't about to participate in the life lesson.

Along with mentally scripting next week's menus, Annika studies Carl to try to grasp a hint as to how she might gain his cooperation. No matter how much effort the hassled mother exerts, it doesn't work and so they continue struggling all the way out of the store.

~

Later that evening, Carl moves stealthily past the boldly colored "KEEP OUT" sign that guards his bedroom door. He quietly walks the length of the upstairs hall to the door leading to their third floor attic. Although the rest of his family is involved in other projects, alone he moves cautiously, throwing furtive glances over his shoulder making sure no one is watching him.

The youngest Williams child climbs the steep, sometimes creaky steps and enters the large attic. As he approaches the magnificent train set, his eyes sparkle with emotions that he can't describe. At first he gently rearranges the train cars and scenery pieces but, before long, begins handling them roughly.

Once in the privacy of this family fantasyland, his face lights up as a strange faraway look falls over his pale, marble-like face. Appearing to be in somewhat of a trance, Carl stays to play much longer than he intends.

⌒ *19* ⌒

The night is dark in a dreary, run-down part of town. Trash lines the streets that run parallel to the time worn, commercial railroad tracks.

Inside a flea-bitten motel room a small, disheveled woman lies on a filthy bed where the hypodermic needle she just pumped into her vein still hangs from her arm. Instantly her eyes roll back into her head and her mouth gapes open. Although her irregular breaths are barely audible, they are deep and ragged.

A scream splits the silence. A light from a blinking, neon "MOT L" sign reveals a cardboard box perched precariously on top of a chest of drawers in a room that time forgot. Unrelenting, heartbreaking screams rise from within the box.

Inside the paper enclosure, a frantic, squalling infant with a blue face and extremities stiff with rage flails at the sides of the cardboard crib. A filthy bottle lies empty beside him, out of reach of his immature grasp. His sagging, heavy diaper is saturated with urine and his thin, wiry body is smeared with dried feces.

The infant continues to howl a most haunting scream as the room begins to shake around him. Bright lights from the window flash on and off with the rhythm of a passing train while lonely train whistles obliterate the baby's shrieks.

Completely weak, but using all her might, the woman comes to and struggles to rise from the bed. She finally staggers across the room, cautiously holds the door open a sliver and looks furtively all around before moving a muscle. Then, as if shot from a cannon, she suddenly flees from the room, leaving the door gaping wide open and letting the chilly wind into the motel.

The room shakes as each train clamors by, while the infant child screams at the top of his voice. But like trees that fall unnoticed in the forest, his screams go unheeded in the night.

~

Although Carl claims that he doesn't especially like trains, he is inexplicably drawn to them. He stoically guards the truth about the frequent visits that he makes to the family attic in spite of any agreements made with Zeb.

Today, as usual, Carl plays alone and leans heavily against the makeshift table. Thoughtfully, he steps back from the table holding the power switches in his hand. He stalls, all motion suspended for the length of several deep breaths. Then, with great resolve, he suddenly flips the central switch box to full power and watches with great intensity as the trains rush toward one another.

Every muscle in Carl's slim body strains as he awaits impact. When the anticipated head-on collision occurs, the young boy laughs a long, cold laugh that he can't hear because his sinister response is drowned out by the sounds of train whistles screeching through his head.

≈ *20* ≈

When supper is finished, Annika and most of her brood retire to the kitchen to clean up their mess. Annika washes the dishes while Jarren dries. And Lexi, free from other chores at the moment, sits at the kitchen table surrounded by her homework assignments.

Jarren holds a wet dish up to show his mother and says quietly, "It's still dirty."

Annika shrugs and grins at her son and playfully quips, "Good dish dryers take up the slack when stuff gets missed."

When Lexi hears that, she looks up from her books. "Carl doesn't do that," the girl interjects.

"Carl doesn't do what?" the mother wonders aloud.

Lexi continues, "He doesn't make things look good."

Her face screws up in a big frown. "What do you mean by that, Honey?" Annika asks.

Jarren joins into the conversation, "He doesn't cooperate. With us anyway."

Annika remains silent but looks at both her children with obvious interest.

"He does whatever he wants, but not what you want," Jarren continues.

"Like what?" the mother asks. "Give me an example."

Lexi is somewhat uncomfortable tattling, as they sometimes call such reporting, but understands that sometimes it's important to join in the conversation. For a moment she speaks with a little too much enthusiasm. "He doesn't make his bed and has dirty stuff everywhere."

"His room stinks," Jarren adds.

On a roll, the adolescent girl adds, "And when you're not here he's mean to us."

Suddenly hungry, Lexi walks to the cupboard and takes a box of Jell-O off the shelf. The box is closed but the inside wrapper is folded neatly and the box is completely empty. Lexi shakes the box, peers into it again, and when she sees nothing, throws the package away. She sits back down with a puzzled look on her face.

Annika is unaware of Lexi's activity and continues, "He's new to our family so it'll take time for him to get used to our ways."

Still part of the conversation, Lexi wonders, "Mama, did you notice that he calls you Annika?"

Jarren added his observation, "Yeah, that's true except when he wants something."

⁀ *21* ⁀

Although she doesn't want to, it's hard for Annika not to notice that Zeb and Carl seem to spend a lot of time together. Today they've have their heads together all afternoon fixing things and putting Carl's bike back together in the garage. Both speak softly as they paint and oil things, as they do 'guy things' together.

To an outsider it almost looks like the pair is in cahoots, or at least that's how it sometimes seems to Annika when she feels left out. Like now.

Carl excitedly points at the bike and exclaims, "This'll be so cool!"

Zeb happily agrees, "Yeah, way cool!"

The boy almost gushes, "I'm so glad you're helping me with this, Dad."

Always guided by an internal need to help Carl adapt to their family, Zeb cautions,

"No, problem, Son. I'm glad to do it with you. But you know you'll need to take care of your bike and put it away when you're not using it."

"Right, I will!" he almost shouts with glee.

Annika enters the garage wiping her wet hands on her apron and smiling broadly at 'her men,' as she lovingly calls them. "Supper time, guys," she informs them.

Carl scowls at her and explosively states, "Aww, shit. Can't you see we're busy?"

Zeb is taken aback by Carl's attitude and bristles at the boy for the first time. "That's unacceptable! Don't talk to your mother that way!"

Upon hearing the new, unfamiliar tones in his father's voice, the boy backs down quickly, "Sorry, Daddy."

On their way into the house Carl turns his head so Zeb can't see his face and flashes Annika a twisted "I won" sort of smile.

Annika gives Carl the space his behavior demands.

⚞ *22* ⚟

It's a sunny day, great for working among the flowers as Annika, deep in thought, loves to do. Annika digs furiously in the dirt, her face almost contorted by the concentration.

After a day at his ministerial duties Zeb returns home and spies his bride completely engrossed and partially covered in soil while tending her green things, as he calls her flowers. Pleased to have time to relax and be with the her, Zeb crosses the lawn to say hello.

Annika gets a glimpse of him out of the corner of her eye. Something burns its way through her mind so she doesn't wait until her husband reaches her. She nearly blurts out, "I think Carl has problems that are bigger than me."

By the time Zeb reaches her with a 'Well, hello' smile, he is puzzled. "What's going on?" he wonders out loud.

She knows she sounds almost paranoid, but at this point Annika can't quit. The woman suddenly feels embarrassed about her impulsive approach and speaking so frankly outside their bedroom.

Annika goes on, "I don't know how to get close to him. When I give him a hug, I get hurt because he kicks my shins or steps on my feet. Things like that." Still embarrassed about bringing this up, she continues anyway. "He says they're accidents, but I wonder."

Somewhat bewildered, Zeb sits down beside her and speaks without considering the impact his words will have on Annika. "He's always polite and full of smiles around me."

She nods, "Yes, I can see that he is and that makes me crazy!"

"You sound jealous. That's not at all like you, Annika," he responds.

The bewildered woman shakes her head and denies, "I don't think I'm jealous. I just wish he were that sweet to me, too."

Trying to figure things out, Zeb ventures a guess. "Maybe you're a little too hard on him."

She shrugs sadly and agrees that might be possible and replies, "Well, something is going on, that's for sure."

Remembering how much he loves her and not wanting to be unkind to the love of his life, Zeb adds, "I think you just may have a bit of an overactive imagination, Baby."

She takes that as a sign their conversation is over for today, so gets up on her feet. Aware of the silent message, Zeb gets up and reaches out to take her gloved hand in his. He looks deeply at her with soft eyes and slowly removes her dirty old gardening glove. The gentle man holds her hand up to his then links their baby fingers in a child-like gesture of love.

Annika is touched by her husband's tenderness and offers him a loving smile even though she's sure that's not the last word about Carl's behaviors.

She still wonders and worries no matter how hard she tries not to.

⁀ *23* ⁀

She has always loved baking bread, but Annika especially loves the smell of the dough and the feel of it in her hands. She stands at the kitchen counter kneading a large, fragrant mound and, as usual, is really into it. As she rolls and flops the dough on the cutting board, she's too busy to remember that every time she bakes her nose itches relentlessly. Today is no different, so flour has somehow crept up her arms and onto her face.

Jarren wanders into the kitchen looking somewhat preoccupied, a look that disturbs his mother. "Mmmmm, that smells good," he says halfheartedly.

With a warm smile at her first born, Annika states, "It'll be ready by supper. Hungry?"

Jarren barely nods and replies uncomfortably, "Ma, Tito asked me to eat supper at his house tonight."

Disappointed, she speaks so as not to give her feelings away, "Oh, okay."

When Jarren remains silent, Annika finds that unusual and is puzzled so explores further, "Lexi is spending the night with Kate tonight, too. Was there anything special going on at school today that I should know about?"

Noncommittally, her son shakes his head and says, "Huh-uh, not that I know of."

Jarren silently wanders out of the room leaving Annika to wonder what is going on with her family. Her arms grow tired as she pounds on the dough.

The phone rings and when Annika answers she's pleased to hear her friend Mary on the other end. She has an idea what the phone call is all about, so, with a pleasant voice, Annika says, "Is it time for our monthly meeting already? My how time flies."

With a good deal of understanding Mary talks to the worried mom in a kind way. "It's been a while since I've seen you. I'm sure breaking in new kids takes lots of time. How's it going?"

Although Mary can't see her face, Annika is suddenly keenly aware of changes within her family and feels strangely protective of them, so carefully selects her words. Needing sugar for her baking project, Annika takes the box of sugar from the cupboard as she talks and frowns when she finds the box closed tightly but completely empty. Not able to focus on two things, her baking and the conversation at once, she absentmindedly tosses the box in the trash.

Masking any turmoil, Annika replies, "Every thing is just fine. Thanks."

Not sure she's buying it, but unwilling to press the issue, Mary responds casually, "I'm glad to hear that. I knew you wouldn't have any trouble with that darling boy." She pauses to take a breath before changing the topic. "Well, the ladies from church are meeting for lunch this week? Will you join us?"

Apologetic, Annika says slowly, "Not this month, Mary. You know how frantic the lives of pastor's wives can get. But thanks for asking."

≈ *24* ≈

When all else fails to console her soul, Annika knows she can always go outside and enjoy the fresh air and sunshine. Ever since she was a child sitting beside her mother and tending their flowers, she's found solace in nature.

Today is similar and while her hands fly, her mind flits about like a butterfly who touches down here and there. Among the rapid movement in her brain, she remembers that sometimes she just needs to leave some topics alone. And then there are other worries that she needs to turn over to her Maker in hopes that solutions to them will occur to her sooner than later.

Her garden supplies and hose lay on the ground near Annika as she kneels and digs with a vengeance. Almost frantic, she seems to be trying to work out some unseen frustrations as she tills.

Slowly, slowly she creeps her way along the flowerbed, tidying under the bushes toward the back of her thick, luscious garden. Annika reaches into the mound of flowers with her spade and as the tool strikes resistance, a surprised look crosses her face and she stops digging.

Confused and dumbstruck, Annika slowly moves the dead leaves aside with her hand tool. The movement exposes a new heap of dirt that looks to her like a shallow grave. She cautiously reaches her gloved hand into the pile and retrieves what she thinks might be the remains of several birds. Annika is horrified.

The bones she examines look twisted, broken and blackened. Maybe they've been burned, she thinks. Annika's heart feels heavy and like it's slamming against the inside of her chest. With increasing emotions she falls back on her elbows as she attempts to control her ragged breaths.

∿

The makeshift table in the attic remains stands alone in its assigned place. The scenery, including the hills and tunnels, appears untouched.

Unknown to the Williams family, however, the metal engines and railway cars are crushed and twisted and have been left in an angry, mangled mess.

⇜ *25* ⇝

After twenty years of marriage Annika and Zeb have established several bedtime routines, practices that have kept the love bonds strong between them. They usually retire at the same time in the evening even though once behind closed doors they aren't always ready to sleep. Their time to unwind, to process daily activities, or just to be together has always been considered sacrosanct, a time devoted only to each other.

Because of their history Zeb is surprised to see Annika already in bed and perhaps, he thinks, pretending to be asleep. He speaks quietly just in case his love really is sleeping. "I didn't know you were here."

Without moving a muscle she says groggily, "I needed time alone."

He looks at her closely in an attempt to determine the truth. "Are you having a problem?"

"Never!" she responds sarcastically, her voice muffled by the covers pulled up to her nose.

Zeb leans down to look into her eyes but she closes them, refusing to reveal her angst. "Tell me, Annika," he says softly.

She barely stirs. "You don't want to hear this."

Knowing that taking on a negative attitude won't help anything, so when he says, "How do you know that?" Zeb tries not to sound defensive.

She speaks with a force he's rarely heard from her, "Because I've tried telling you before, Zebediah."

From her tone and the use of his full name, he immediately grasps the seriousness of this exchange. With fear clutching at his throat, he fights to stay calm. "What are you saying?"

Annika looks away quickly, but not before Zeb sees the fear from her heart reflected in her eyes. "Is it Carl?" he asks cautiously, hoping against hope that he's wrong.

Annika nods slowly, surely. He tries to follow her comments, but no matter how hard he prays he can't anticipate her next words. Zeb remains silent but his emotions make him feel like his heart is about to burst through his chest wall.

After moments of an expectant silence, with restrained emotions Annika spills her thoughts, "I'm told I'm too hard on him, that I imagine what I see or that I expect too much..."

Zeb starts to speak but Annika charges on with increasing emotions. "I think," the distraught woman continues, "that he's tired, or not used to me yet." With slight hesitation, and just above a whisper, she says, "Or he's just plain lost to us."

He blurts, "But I don't have a problem with him."

Annika is aghast and a look of total disbelief is etched deeply into her face. She proclaims hoarsely, "We live with a wrecking ball and you can't see it."

Summoning all the empathy he can muster, Zeb gets close to her and says softly, "Sweetheart, is it possible you overestimate the problems?"

If Annika has ever been presented with the opportunity to sneer in her life, this is that moment. Filled with disgust which startles her, she says, "There it is, that attitude, that blame. It's no wonder I feel like I'm a bad mom."

Annika rolls into a ball and turns her back on Zeb for the first time in their married life. He is left to ponder what he has said wrong.

⤳ *26* ⤳

Annika hasn't been able to find much peace lately, so she is especially pleased to look for some at her sewing machine. Over the years she's found that making personal homemade items for her family provides her with time to pray and to create.

For her, creating something from a little nothing happens when she keeps her heart open to what her Maker is trying to tell her. When life gets bumpy for her, sitting quietly and listening to music helps get her centered and releases some of the worry that fills her heart.

When she works around the house, Annika often hums to the oldies, a trait that her children both love and tease her about. Today, her usual monotone has a hint of a lilt to it, that is, until she hears the voice of a news reporter break through the music.

With some uncharacteristic excitement in his voice the radio announcer exclaims, "We interrupt this programming to bring you a special news report."

Annika stops sewing to listen intently and whispers, "Oh, God," prayerfully.

The announcer continues, "Police Chief Joel reports a local thirteen-year-old was found early this morning at Pioneers Park. The girl is fighting to survive multiple knife wounds and is in serious condition at Lincoln Hospital."

Distressed, Annika moves closer to the radio so she doesn't miss a word.

"Her identity," the reporter goes on, "is being withheld until the family has been notified. However, if you know anything about it or notice anything unusual please call LPD immediately."

Totally distraught, and with no understanding of her feelings, Annika bolts from the room, runs down the stairs and outside, unsure of where she's going. Or why.

≈ *27* ≈

It's cleaning day at the Williams' household. Even though Annika isn't all that fond of vacuuming, she goes over the entire house every Thursday, rain or shine. Her ancient cannister vacuum was a wedding gift from old, practical Aunt Libby and although it takes more energy than the new self-propelled kind, it still works great.

By the time she gets to the second floor hall, she's broken a sweat. Every week she thinks it's time for her kids to practice using the decrepit machine, but she just hasn't yet gotten around to the transfer of power, as she thinks of it.

Intent on capturing every piece of lint or stray fuzzy, she's in a zone and concentrating deeply. Well, that is until she gets hit by a wall of stink.

"What the heck?" Annika says as she looks around to discover the odor is more intense just outside Carl's room. The mother suddenly remembers that their initial ritual of tucking him in nightly ended weeks ago and she realizes she hasn't been in Carl's room for a while now.

As she pushes past the "KEEP OUT" sign on Carl's bedroom door the stink gets worse. Her sudden tears, mixed with the fumes of rancid garbage, sting the inside of her eyelids.

When the door is open enough to enter, Annika's eyes open wide in shock. She's met with mounds of garbage and so much filth that she hesitates to touch anything or take another step.

"Oh, my gosh!" she exclaims under her breath.

The room looks ransacked to her. Smelly clothes are everywhere with trash and half-eaten food mixed in with Carl's laundry. Although she's not sure why, Annika lifts the corner of Carl's mattress to find layers of trash sandwiched between the mattress and box spring. His copy of "Tales from the Grave" is wrapped in plastic along with used candy wrappers, empty cereal boxes, flat Jell-o boxes and cookie remains.

On the far wall on the other side of Carl's bed she sees smears of brownish matter and is truly afraid to explore the situation. But before she gathers the courage to move, a foul smell of feces and urine from his bed sheets reaches her nose. Annika is overcome with nausea and is able to take only shallow, panting breaths.

Her anger has been rising in her chest since the moment she opened Carl's bedroom door. She explodes with, "How dare he!" The strong feelings she's feeling for the first time scare her almost more than the situation before her.

At that moment Jarren walks by, but then he comes back to stand in the doorway, staring in disbelief. Working to stay calm since it wouldn't be good for both of them react in anger, the adolescent benignly says, "I'll get the trash bags."

When Jarren returns, he already has gloves on and hands a pair to Annika to protect her hands. They begin furiously tossing trash and garbage into the plastic bags. They work silently, in unison, as they remove the mattress and throw the garbage away. Annika, however, makes sure Carl's book from his birth mother is put away for safe keeping.

Unexpectedly, Annika spies a heart shaped locket among the rubble. When she lifts it to eye level to examine it, a look of surprise crosses her face. Without much thought the woman drops it into the front pocket of her jeans and keeps going.

As quickly as her anger erupts, Annika is overcome with a sadness she's never before experienced in her life.

Suddenly, Carl reaches the doorway of his room and instantly his rage engulfs every fiber of his body. "What the hell are you doing?" he screams.

Fighting to remain calm, she responds in a husky, throaty voice, "Helping you."

Carl becomes frantic and unable to remain still or in one place. He screams louder, "Don't touch my stuff. I don't need your help."

Not sure what to say, Annika hesitates then says, "That's not how it looks to me."

He closes the gap between them and puffs up his chest like wild animals do to ward off their foes, but stops with his face mere inches from Annika's.

In his biggest, deepest threatening voice he hisses, "Get the fuck outta my room and gimme my stuff back. Now!"

On some visceral level Annika knows this is not the moment to back down from her disturbed child. Determined to hold her ground, she pushes her luck and replies with a response full of feeling. "I'll think about it." She holds up several bills in her hand, waves them, and asks, "But first, is this money you stole from me?"

Carl loses it. He flails about and swings at the air near her ears and body. So far he hasn't landed a punch, but as scattered as her thoughts are in the middle of this melee, Annika wonders if the misses are intentional or just a fortunate accident.

Carl seems not to notice and is so rageful he can barely spit out his words. "I didn't steal crap from you! I earn any money I get as your personal slave. Besides, I saw Lexi take money from your purse."

Carl's eyes are cold slits, his rage white hot. With fists clenched he reaches for her, but she responds by pulling herself up to her full height and gives him her own steely-eyed 'I dare you' mother looks.

Ever the protector, Jarren bristles in a way no one has ever observed before and begins to move in Annika's direction. Suddenly Carl screams unintelligibly and bolts from the room, acting like a wild animal. Still out of control, he kicks the walls with every step and slams the door as he blasts his way out of the house.

As quickly as the incident between them started, their home is suddenly and deafeningly silent.

⁓ *28* ⁓

Toward the end of their day Annika and Zeb sit at the dining room table long after dinner is done and their kids have disbursed to their rooms. It's apparent by the way they're leaning into each other, and the damp tissue in Annika's hands, that the topic is serious. As happens more often lately, as the pair chats quietly Annika's tears begin to flow.

Zeb frowns and says, "I'm sorry, Honey, but this is all so hard for me to believe."

Put off by his attitude, Annika asks, "So you think I'm making it up?"

"No, Darling. Not at all," he says with his anxiety level rising. "But do you really believe Carl could have killed Lady?"

She looks hard at her husband through tear-filled eyes. Her steady gaze clearly answers Zeb's question.

Appalled at the idea, Zeb reacts, "My brain just can't grasp the idea of our son harming anyone."

"Let's settle this once and for all." Annika proposes, "How about we ask him?"

"Right here? Right now?" Zeb wonders aloud.

"Why not?" she asks with surprise.

For a few seconds Zeb quietly ponders the issue at hand. He then gets up and walks to the bottom of the stairs and calls, "Carl, come down here."

It sounds like the young boy stomps his way down the stairs then walks to the dining room looking for his dad.

Zeb wastes no time and as he directs Carl to sit down. He speaks directly to him. "We have something to discuss with you. Your mother and I have been talking about Lady and how much we miss her."

"That was sad," Carl responds quickly. "What happened to her, anyway?"

Nearly gritting her teeth, Annika screws up her courage. "That's what we'd like to know, too."

The youngster suddenly appears tense but looks directly into Annika's eyes. Almost glaring at her he says, "Why ask me? What about Jarren or Lexi? Maybe they know."

Sticking with the conversation, Zeb states, "We want to ask you."

Carl takes a deep breath and appears to calm down almost immediately. He intentionally looks directly at both parents, first at Zeb then at Annika, but says nothing.

Annika works hard to screw up her courage and asks directly, "Carl, did you hurt Lady?"

He still looks directly into her eyes. Annika thinks Carl looks almost peaceful, which doesn't make sense under the circumstances.

"What do you think?" he says with a challenging tone.

Without hesitation Annika responds, "That you know more than you're telling."

Sounding almost lawyer-like, Carl says, "Did you see me do it?"

Suddenly curious, Zeb reacts with, "Do what, Carl? Did we see you do what?"

The boy backs down a bit then answers, "Whatever happened to Lady."

Meaning to encourage, Annika invites Carl, "Just be honest."

Carl appears insulted and nearly screams, "I am!"

"Did you kill her?" Zeb presses.

Carl jumps up from his chair and fights to keep from losing his cool. "Whenever stuff happens around here I always get blamed."

Remaining calm, Annika wants the problem to get resolved, so she takes a risk. "I think you did it, Carl."

He plants his feet into the floor. As Carl thinks, his hateful glare nearly pierces Annika's soul. Suddenly his voice becomes soft and controlled. With venom dripping from his tongue he simply says, "Prove it."

Frowning, Zeb tries to track their convoluted conversation with Carl and wonders aloud, "So you did it?"

Appearing innocent to the core, Carl takes on a different tone with his father. "No, Daddy, I didn't hurt her. You've got to believe me."

Suddenly concerned that he and Annika were being too hard on the boy, Zeb walks to him and gives Carl a quick hug. "Enough for today," he says and releases Carl to leave the room.

Stunned by Zeb's last action, Annika slumps in her chair. Unable to comprehend Carl's reaction and Zeb's willingness to let their son off the hook, Annika feels finally and totally defeated.

🖛 *29* 🖚

It's late night and Annika sits alone in the kitchen, her favorite room in the house. An ignored book lies in her lap, open to a page unfamiliar to her. It's easy to see past the uncombed hair that her eyes aren't focusing even in the unusually darkened room. With rumpled clothes and dark circles under her eyes she feels like she exists only in a scary place deep inside her own head.

She's been siting like a stone for nearly an hour before Zeb enters the room dressed in his pajamas. He looks at the clock and sees it's already 11:15. By now Annika is normally ready to sleep and the change frightens him. The lines around his eyes deepen with worry.

"Anni, are you coming to bed soon?" he asks softly.

Not moving a muscle, Annika keeps staring into space. When she stays silent

Zeb moves closer, stands near and looks at her hard. His concern turns to desperation. Squatting down to get into her line of vision, Zeb pleads, "Baby?"

He knows that the sound of his voice has reached her ears because she slowly drops her head onto the back of her hand that lies lifeless on the table. She waves him away with the other.

He's dumbfounded by what's going on with his beloved Annika and stands immobile for what seems like hours. Zeb tries to decide what he can or should do to help her and finally decides to let her be for now. He leaves the room.

After several more minutes of hiding in plain sight Annika slowly pulls herself up and leans heavily on the table for balance. With some resolve etched on her face, she reaches into one of the upper cupboards and removes a bottle of liquor that was a gift from Uncle Ned last Christmas. She uncaps the bottle, pours several splashes into a glass she takes from the dish drainer, and gulps down the warming liquid.

Unused to alcoholic beverages, Annika chokes, coughs and clears her throat before returning to her seat at the table. She places the bottle in front of her with a clear intention of having more.

The liquor's initial effect calms her down so Annika starts sipping the potion straight. Although her vision is blurry, eventually she squints up at the clock and notices that it's after one in the morning. Now, slumped in her chair, she know she is messier than she's ever been in her entire life, but tonight she just doesn't care.

She really can't focus her eyes now, but because she and Zeb have lived their entire married life in this house, she knows every inch by heart. When she stumbles out of the kitchen and up the stairs to their bedroom, she's noisy but luckily knows the way intimately so doesn't cause any harm to her feet and shins.

Annika is totally intoxicated for the first time in her life so is especially clumsy as she opens the door to their room. In her drunken state she stumbles to her side of the bed and falls into bed next to a man she no longer knows.

Still in the same clothes, she passes out as soon as her head hits the pillow so doesn't see that Zeb is awake and so full of fear that he's been struck dumb.

⌐ *30* ⌐

The next day Annika is still sluggish and tries to pretend all is well as she mops the kitchen floor and wipes down the counters. She decides the chores are a contrition of sorts. After filling a bag with trash from cleaning the refrigerator, she sits it on a kitchen chair and secures the opening with a tie.

She thinks for a moment then walks to the dining room door and calls out, "Carl, come and help me."

After only stone silence from his direction, she tries again. "Carl! Please come here."

After several moments the boy noisily enters the kitchen letting her know how perturbed he is about having his activity interrupted. Carl slaps the table and kicks the chairs across the room with well placed kicks.

"What?" he demands.

With great restraint Annika attempts to ignore his foul mood and bites the sides of her tongue to keep her from being rude to him. She knows taking an attitude with him will not help the situation.

She looks directly at Carl and says assertively, "Honey, take the trash out for me."

Annika blinks hard and is startled when her child gets in her face and growls his response, "Why me? I'm busy!"

Instinctively knowing the importance of not reacting to his anger and holding him responsible, she steels herself as she speaks softly, "Please, Carl."

The youth angrily spins away from her, grabs the trash bag, swings it through the air and then drop kicks it.

"Carl, no!" the frustrated mother nearly shouts.

Annika can see that although his body is there wildly stomping on the trash, his mind is somewhere else. As much as she cares for this troubled child, it is not possible for her to hear sounds of an approaching freight train that's roaring its way through his psyche. The guttural sounds coming from Carl's mouth make this human child sound like a wounded animal.

Annika tries to redirect him without physically intervening saying, "Calm down. It's just trash." Her efforts don't work and by now Carl is in a frenzy and completely out of control. Annika is so stunned she fearfully moves to the side of the room to get out of harm's way.

The kitchen surfaces that were clean from Annika's earlier efforts are now totally covered with garbage and trash. As quickly as it started, the barrage ends, at least for the moment, and the stomping and flailing appear to be done.

He peers around the room with a look of confusion, unsure of what has just happened. Believing he's had no part in the wreckage, Carl decides that Annika made him mad and had instigated the whole nasty scene.

Unwilling to accept responsibility for his actions he pulls himself up to his full height to distract Annika's view of the surprise on his face. On his way across the room Carl hesitates a moment then tries to shoot Annika dead with a bone chilling glare before slamming his way out of the kitchen door.

⌒ *31* ⌒

In a dark corner of the city park leaves from the summer trees block out most of the light from the few streetlights placed around the perimeter of the park. Other than the hum of cars at a distance and the slight rustling of the leaves, all is quiet.

In the dim moonlight the movement of two bodies can be seen on one of the picnic tables in the area. Dark music accompanies the writhing which keeps the beat and matches the head-banging tunes coming from an MP3 player nearby.

Suddenly the sounds of love change when a quick flash of light bounces off a shiny metal object. A muffled scream is emitted from the bottom of the sweaty heap.

The wiry body on top lets out guttural sounds that are indistinguishable from anything human. Suddenly, the clacking of charging train wheels wipe out any other sounds coming from the park.

A male voice utters, "You fucking cow!"

Deep shadows obliterate the view, but the bodies begin moving more rapidly. The body on top swings his arms in irregular movements and his body glistens as he makes hissing sounds.

A male voice hisses, "Fucking whore."

"No! Please!" a female voice pleads.

The train sounds clack faster than before while a train whistle obliterates deafening screams.

His voice changes to deep and raspy. "You're a fucking bitch just like the rest of them."

Unexpectedly, all movements stop. The entire area is bathed in silence except for the sound of running footfalls. And the whimpering sounds of a girl in pain.

⌒ *32* ⌒

Like a team in cahoots, Zeb and Lexi attach streamers and balloons to doors, walls and windows around the dining room. As if by design they had enough left to decorate around the chocolate sheet cake Jarren places in the middle of the table.

The three have noticed changes in Annika and they miss her terribly. The trio wants to help pull her from the depths of the personal hell she's been living in lately, so they are all excited today.

Lexi uses a stage whisper that always cracks them up, "Daddy, do you think Mama knows?"

Zeb shakes his head emphatically. "We're world-class secret keepers."

Lexi is thrilled to be able to pull this off without being discovered.

Zeb added, "Besides, she's worried about Carl and might not notice what we're up to."

Jarren's ears perk up. "Where is he?"

Their preoccupied father doesn't want to go there right now so just says, "I don't know, but today is for Mom. We'll deal with other issues later."

The front doorbell rings, and they can hear the hushed women's voices coming from the other side of the front door. Annika's friends, Mary, Lee, and Carol, from their church and neighborhood enter cheerfully and hand their gifts for Annika to Lexi.

Lee and Carol nod in agreement as Jarren stands post at the living room door. Lexi busies herself looking for the right spot to put her mother's gifts.

Carol adds, "We've missed her at our social hours."

"Today we make up for lost time," Zeb declares.

Smart aleck Lee clarifies, "We're celebrating the ninth anniversary of number twenty-nine, right?"

They all laugh and Zeb encourages them with a "That's the spirit!"

A preoccupied Annika, dressed in clean casual clothes and shirt, walks into their nicely decorated living room and plants herself firmly in her favorite chair.

The celebrating party doesn't give her time to do anything else as they all rush into the room shouting, "Surprise!" and "Happy Birthday!" Annika startles and takes a few moments to focus her eyes on the guests and figure out what's happening. Her face changes from expressionless to support a somewhat hollow laugh.

"Sneaks, all of you!" Annika proclaims.

Zeb can't help himself as he looks at her with pent up longing. While he's sorely missed her and suddenly gets misty, he manages to say, "We are good, aren't we?"

As soon as the adults sit down, Lexi is ready to get this party going and begins bringing the gifts to Annika. She chats and laughs while she opens gifts, pleased to be remembered.

Zeb manages to sit next to Annika, a simple pleasure that's been missing from their lives recently. He inconspicuously touches her arm, hand and hair any chance he has and sighs deeply. He begins thinking that the tough phase they've been experiencing recently might be over now.

Annika thanks everyone as she opens the gifts for her. Then they chatter and move into the dining room to enjoy the treat Jarren's made for them. As Lee serves cake and ice cream, each Williams family member pays close attention to Annika's needs. Unlike many recent days, Annika smiles often in response to the attentive spirits of this day.

Unexpectedly, they hear the front door slam against the wall nearby and look at each other in dismay. All is quiet as they listen to footsteps cross the living room and, suddenly, Carl appears in the dining room doorway.

Annika sits as still as a post, stunned and speechless. Zeb, Jarren and Lexi share a common expression, one of confusion. The women are perplexed and look from face to face trying to get a clue about what is happening in front of them.

Carl is full of ear-to-ear smiles as he slowly, almost cautiously, approaches Annika. "Here," he says as he hands her a homemade, loving-hands-at-home envelope.

Annika has not yet blinked and her bulging eyes resemble a deer in the headlights, like they could pop out of their sockets any second. She's fearful and, like the others, can't take her eyes off Carl. Annika reluctantly reaches out for the envelope he's still offering, and she suspiciously opens it, one flap at a time.

Carl continues to stand stiffly in front of her. "Happy Birthday, Mama," he says with that Cheshire-cat-kinda-grin.

The overwhelmed mother reads the card slowly. In seconds she begins to weep in a cry that would alter her voice if she spoke. Annika silently hands the card to Zeb for him to read aloud.

The furrows in Zeb's face deepen as he reads the handwritten words, "Mommy, I love you with all my heart. Love, Carl."

Annika remains speechless. Jarren and Lexi are speechless. Lee, Mary and Carol get tears in their eyes at the sweet sentiment.

Zeb, puzzled, looks from face to face, stiffens, and says, "You sure outdid yourself this time, Carl."

Carl puffs up displaying all the characteristics usually seen in one who's full of self pride. He still smiles that rare toothy grin and looks deeply into everyone's eyes except one. He avoids Annika's gaze.

$\sim$

Later that night, in the privacy of their own room, Annika is dressed in her nightgown and stands brushing her teeth at the bathroom sink. She studies her own face and body in the mirror as Zeb enters the bathroom. She glances sideways at him but then quickly looks away. Knowing that she's not going to make eye contact, although he doesn't know why, he watches her intently with a soft, glowing look on his face.

Zeb states softly, "Sometimes I forget how beautiful you are."

She pauses, gives him a fleeting glance then keeps brushing her teeth, almost steeling herself from Zeb's comment.

Understanding when it's time to change the subject, but still not knowing why, he tries again, "Are you glad all our kids are home?"

With no change in expressions, Annika rinses her mouth then grabs her hairbrush and brushes her hair.

When Zeb doesn't get the response he hopes for or a clue about what's wrong, he soon gets frustrated. Eventually though, he tries again. "Okay, so I'm a louse."

Annika carefully places her brush on the counter and leaves the bathroom. When she arrives at her side of the bed, she pulls the covers back and climbs into bed facing the wall without one word or change in her expression.

Limp with sadness, Zeb concludes, "I see you're not talking to me tonight."

"G'night, Zeb," she says in a monotone.

⌐ *33* ⌐

Sitting at the kitchen table in clothes she usually saves for working in her garden, Annika writes checks from their checkbook. While she pays bills she finishes her quick-start cup of coffee for the day.

Dressed for church, Zeb enters the room and although he anticipates a chilly reception, bends over and plants a noisy kiss on her cheek anyway. "Have a great day, Anni," he says with a lilt in his voice and heads for the back door.

She nods at him and offers him a wan smile as he leaves, the first in several days, which is appreciated by her husband. Then Annika glances at the television playing from on the kitchen counter, looks at the bills before her, and then back to the TV.

Even alone with her own company Annika becomes visibly tense.

The TV anchor states with urgency in his voice, "...Captain Joel reports there are similar injures. This victim and the first girl were both stabbed, both are thirteen, and Lincoln Junior High students."

Annika is gripped with fear and fights to control the tears that spring to her eyes and feel like they're searing the inside of her eyelids.

The TV anchor continues, "It is believed these two incidents may be related. With serious injuries, both girls have miraculously survived the attacks. Stay tuned for more information at ten tonight."

The woman at the kitchen table shrinks and becomes immovable, staring hard at the air. Annika's brain whirs as she tries to make sense of the newest pieces of a puzzle that's occurring around her.

⇌ *34* ⇋

Putting on their best faces this morning, Annika, Jarren and Lexi sit somberly in a front row of the Rock Solid Holiness Baptist Church where Pastor Williams is about to preach. Carl sits with the youth among the choir and Annika notices some sneaky moves as he periodically pokes at the kids near him. While the church fills to capacity this morning, Zeb greets members of his congregation at the door and the organist plays welcoming, upbeat organ pieces. When the organist finishes the hymn, Zeb steps up to the pulpit and speaks with a godly tone in his voice.

"Today," he says, "after the injuries of two of our beloved young ladies from this community, we prepare to battle the evil that walks among us."

Rose, Carl's caseworker, suddenly enters through the front doors, rushing because she doesn't like being late, and selects a seat behind Annika and the children. She says, "Amen. Praise be to God!" in response to the Pastor's message as she sits down.

Zeb continues, "We fight this evil with God's limitless mercy and powerful love! Our days on earth are precious so we must reach out to everyone around us with compassion!"

The congregation murmurs in agreement.

As their pastor's energy builds, he nearly sings out, "We must reach out in love to those in our families, to those in our neighborhoods and even to those strangers He puts in our midst."

Their enthusiastic murmurs grow louder.

Zeb is building to the pinnacle of his sermon. "And yes, we must also offer welcoming arms out to sinners and to those among us who are having difficulties in their lives."

Many members stand, raise their hands and sing their "Amen" in response to their beloved Pastor's words. Annika, Jarren and Lexi behave like this is the first time they've ever heard him preach and the trio is completely enthralled with every word.

"God will protect us," Reverend Williams says with a voice that could reach the heavens, "in our fight for right! Only God in His Mercy and Glory will mend the ways of the wicked!"

He pauses so the parishioners can catch their breaths then concludes, "May the Spirit of Jesus Christ be with us all!"

Now the congregation takes to their feet. Annika, Jarren and Lexi are swept along with the electric current that passes through them as a group and as a family of God. Together their enthusiasm noisily fills the air with wild clapping, and their "Amen" and "Praise be to the Lord," can be heard down the block.

Rose shouts and the other people throughout the church say in unison, "Praise be to God, our Father!"

Zeb is spurred on by the fire in their hearts. "We need this attacker of our young girls to be caught and caught now! Oh, Lord! We pray that our children will be safe so they can go forth into the world to spread Your Holy Word!"

"Amen!" and "Amen!" are muttered and shouted and offered up in the fervent voices of each person witnessing today's sermon.

Reverend Williams is at his finest. "Right now, Ladies and Gentlemen," he continues, "turn to your neighbor and greet them. I want you to offer them peace so all will live as one harmonious family in abundant faith and blessings."

All the members of the congregation affectionately greet their friends and neighbors sitting nearby. Annika and her children do the same while Zeb walks down the center aisle shaking hands and hugging those along the way.

He returns to the pulpit, waits a moment for his flock to quiet down, then speaks sincerely. "As many of you know, the children of this congregation and the Children's Ministry have been an important priority for me. So please, join in with me and let us celebrate our children!"

Their 'Amens' and clapping spur him on, "It's been my constant pleasure serving you wonderful folks here at our beloved Rock Solid Holiness Baptist Church."

The Pastor can't help being full of enthusiasm and looks lovingly at the parishioners and his family sitting at his feet. He gestures toward the choir and speaks with a voice filled with feeling, "Our children are our lifeblood and our future. We must nurture and stubbornly guide them, especially during hard times like we're experiencing now, as well as in abundance."

Although the congregation mutters in undeniable agreement, Annika suddenly becomes uncomfortable and has difficulty making eye contact with her husband.

Caught up in the moment, Zeb doesn't seem to notice what's happening in the front row and goes on. "In their time of need we must not give up on our young ones, because to give up on even one child means we have failed all our children."

Mrs. Cable, one of the original members at Pastor Williams' church stands up, stretches out her hands and shouts, "Glory Be to the Father!"

The adored minister continues. "Let us take a few moments to listen to our wonderful choir sing their praises unto the Lord. And then the Youth Choir will also sing some songs they've been practicing all week. While our choir sends joyful praises to the Heavens, let us remember our young girls and their families in our prayers that they will be protected by our Heavenly Father."

During the singing of several lively hymns most of the children in the youth choir keep their eyes pealed on their director. Carl, however, beams while in the limelight and makes sure everyone's looking at him by exaggerating his smiles and facial expressions.

As everyone in the church listens attentively, they sing and clap along with the music until the choir, followed by the children, finish their songs of praise.

When the singing is completed, Zeb claps then concludes, "Let us also pray for each other as we attempt to live in this moment and in Christ's Grace." Then he adds, "Please join us in the community room right after service for a special Sunday social."

The pastor glances somewhat nervously at Annika as he finishes, hoping against hope that today's sermon has somehow touched her. And maybe warmed her up a bit, too, he thinks.

⤜ *35* ⤛

These days Reverend Williams is obviously at his best and most sure of himself when leading his parish. He joyfully greets the members of his congregation at the door of the community hall while the choir members scurry about hosting the social.

Carl is more gracious than ever before and helps the older parishioners by taking their snacks to the tables for them to enjoy. He even goes a little overboard and helps several older ladies into their seats.

When Zeb sees Annika, he beckons to her and she slowly makes her way to him. Jarren and Lexi join their friends while Annika stands silently near Zeb, but not too near.

She's stunned to see a smiling Carl bring her coffee and cake, right away, and without her asking. Then she's even more perplexed when he stands quietly at her side, as if waiting for her instructions.

Her church friend Vera comes out of the crowd to join her and says, "Nice to see you, Annika. I've heard you've been under the weather and do hope you're feeling better today."

That comment trips Annika's insecurity button and she's unsure how to interpret Vera's comment or how to respond to it. Rather than misspeak, she remains silent, but those around her are deep in conversation so seem not to notice her lack of response.

Undaunted, Vera sticks her hand out to smiling Carl and nearly purrs, "You must be Carl. I've only heard about you so I'm very glad to finally meet you. Nice singing, young man!"

Carl totally beams, "Thank you, Ma'am!" in a voice Annika has never before heard or observed.

Vera makes a gesture that suggests a joining of Annika and Carl and croons, "You're so lucky to have found each other. Are you all settled in now?"

The boy looks at Vera with warm, soft eyes that brighten even more when Rose joins their little circle. He can remain still no longer. "I'm the luckiest kid in town. Aren't I, Mama?"

Annika wonders how to respond without giving away her deep feelings and is relieved when Rose speaks. "You haven't been with them very long, so I certainly am glad to hear that, Carl!"

On a roll, Carl proclaims, "All I want to do is to stay with Mama and Daddy." Then without even a blink he wanders off to find the food.

Rose shares quietly with Annika, "I knew your loving influence would work wonders. Just look at him! He just needed a strong Christian family like yours to turn him around."

The perplexed Annika chooses her words carefully, "He certainly has made a huge difference in my life."

Rose is delighted and says, "Everything sure looks like it's going mighty well."

Annika, having difficulty continuing her charade comments somewhat sarcastically, "There's an old saying about not believing everything you hear and only part of what you see."

Surprised, Rose looks bewildered and remains silent as Annika makes eye contact with someone across the room.

Without ever regaining eye contact with Rose, Annika says, "Excuse me a moment, Rose."

Feeling little awkward when left behind like that, Rose strolls slowly over to Zeb and attempts to start up a conversation. She says to the Reverend, "Carl looks wonderful!"

Zeb nods, giving Rose the indication that he's open to discussing the boy. Zeb confirms it with his enthusiasm, "Yes, and he's interesting, too."

Hoping to get a little more information to satisfy her curiosity, she continues. "Things are going well with him at home?"

"Oh, my, yes," he says as his eyes search the crowd and stop once they find Annika speaking with another parishioner.

Based on his body language and delivery, Rose is not so sure the Pastor is being completely truthful so persists. "And he gets along with the other kids, too?"

The sensitive social worker notices that Zeb stiffens ever so slightly but maintains a pleasant smile on his face and says, "Yes. Yes, he sure does. You did a good job this time too, Rose." After a pause he finishes, "Annika and I are grateful to you."

The line between her brows deepens although she smiles graciously. And then, given a second to think, Rose wonders what is really going on in the Williams' home.

≈ *36* ≈

It's nearly dusk now and the neighborhood is settling down for the evening. The members of the Williams family are all off in their own space doing their own thing. The kids are busily doing homework or at least playing computer games to make it look like they're doing homework. Zeb catches up on the day's news in the living room.

Annika's body can be found slumped in a lawn chair outside on the deck. Her mind is vacant and the final strains of the sunset fall on her absent stare. Wearing yesterday's wardrobe, she either doesn't mind that she looks haggard or she just doesn't realize it. The heart of the Williams family has barely enough energy to bring her glass of watered down tea to her lips.

Soft music wafts over her from inside the house, but Annika doesn't notice. Eventually Jarren wanders out and sits silently beside her. Unsuccessful in his struggle to find words to say to his beloved mother, he finally gives in to his loss of words and just sits. A wave of sadness washes over him and he succumbs to the feelings. He casually wipes the tears that escape from his eyes and then leans over and kisses his mother on the cheek.

His voice is husky with emotion when he speaks. "I'll tell Dad you're out here," he says as he rises slowly and goes into the house.

After Jarren disappears, she closes her eyes and goes far, far away in her head. Silent tears roll down her cheeks.

Zeb stands in the dark just inside the back door watching Annika silently through the screen door. As he moves out to the deck, he feels like an oppressive blanket has been thrown over him. He perches on the edge of the chair next to her without making a sound and just waits for her to speak or something. The truth is, for the first time in his life, he's at a complete loss and isn't even sure what he's waiting for.

Finally he finds his voice and says lovingly, "What's happening to you?"

"Huh?" she startles and blinks at the realization he's there beside her.

All expression is missing from her face and he sees that her eyes look totally blank.

He says with fear gripping his throat, "Where are you?"

"Nowhere," she responds with difficulty.

Zeb drops his head before he says, "I'm a minister with a calling to help people. I wish I could help you..."

She remains motionless with eyes half open, looking toward the horizon.

Zeb continues, "...but you've shut me out."

He thinks he sees Annika gesture sluggishly toward the house before he hears her say thickly, "He's like a boarder in an old-time rooming house. He sleeps in our bed and eats at our table, but we don't really know who he is at all."

The minister who is used to listening to the woes of others decides it's time to listen to his life mate and so invites her to share. "Explain this to me."

Her voice is still groggy, but her words have great meaning to her and Zeb knows that instinctively. She says, "He's not connected to me at all. I don't know why, but I know it deep down inside of me."

He stares at Annika, the woman he used to know but sees now that she's slipped away from him, from all of them, before their unseeing eyes. Out of his own emotional difficulty he stutters uncharacteristically, "Do..., do you want help?"

Annika shakes her head, "It's too late. There's nothing left of me."

Zeb is suddenly terrified for Annika and responds strongly, almost yelling, "What do you mean, there's nothing left?"

With only an ounce of her energy left she states as clearly as she can, "Just what I said. I'm empty, I'm all used up emotionally."

Not wanting to overreact to what he's hearing, Zeb becomes frustrated anyway and tries to grasp what she's trying to tell him.

"It's like," she explains, "I've had the breath kicked out of my lungs and I can't get any air back."

Although he knows any strong reaction is not in his best interest, or in Annika's, he fights the urge to jump and scream. Instead, he says with measured emotions, "By what? You're not making any sense!"

Annika suddenly sits up ramrod straight with an incredulous look on her face. "You mean you don't know?" she sputters. "Where on earth have you been?"

He hesitates in an effort to get a grip on his unexpected emotional surge that's hitting at his chest from inside. He thinks about what to do now, if anything.

A memory crosses his mind and he suddenly, but cautiously, knows what to say. "I know of a woman you might want to talk to."

⌐ *37* ⌐

Annika cautiously enters a door in their local professional building. She is alone and as she pushes the door open she sees many plaques with the name, 'Elizabeth Logan, PhD. A sign inside welcomes her and requests that she complete the initial paperwork that's attached to a clipboard.

The nervous mother completes the forms swiftly then hangs on to them while she waits for the next step. She wanders around the room reading the diplomas on the walls. Sadly, Annika's fears and embarrassment overwhelm her curiosity.

In a few minutes a woman she learns is Elizabeth opens the door to her inner office and beckons her inside. Annika silently hands the papers to the middle aged psychologist who is dressed in a professional looking suit. Her hair has enough gray to soften her facial features and to give her an air of wisdom. Annika also thinks what a beautiful woman she is.

Elizabeth takes the papers from Annika and waits to sit down until Annika selects a soft, overstuffed couch near the window. She sits stiffly then places a pillow from the couch on her lap covering her heart in a protective gesture. While the therapist reads through the paperwork, Annika doesn't know what to say, so says nothing.

It seems like a long wait, but finally Elizabeth lays the papers down, looks gently into her eyes, and says, "I understand you're the mother of a humdinger."

Annika's eyes fly open and she stammers, "A, a what?"

With a soft smile playing on her lips Elizabeth responds, "A humdinger. You know, a wild child."

Almost defensively Annika says, "How do you know that?"

Elizabeth slowly picks up Annika's paperwork and waves it in an easy gesture. "I added two and two and got five."

"Oh," she says dumbly not really understanding but afraid to say so.

Elizabeth says clearly, "History speaks."

Annika frowns, deepening the lines between her brows.

The therapist continues, "You've adopted a couple of kids, with the latest an 11 year old street kid. And more than that, you look shell shocked."

Completely involuntarily, Annika exhibits a hint of a smile on her tense mouth and her eyes become inexplicably misty. She notices that her body relaxes a notch or two as she lets herself lean back against the plush couch. She loosens her grip on the pillow.

Elizabeth prods, "Which one is in trouble? The first?"

The anxious mother responds immediately, "No. No, not Lexi. She's okay."

"Then it's Carl," the psychologist surmises.

Annika nods her head. Elizabeth's directness leaves her disarmed and unprepared with the pat, practiced answers she normally uses to keep from talking about her experiences with Carl.

Elizabeth asks, "Tell me about his history. Any abuse in the past?"

Annika half shrugs and replies, "He came to us from the streets, so we don't know much about his history."

"Who is his social worker," the older woman asks.

Annika responds, "Rose from Children and Family Services."

Elizabeth smiles and nods indicating she knows Rose. "She can help us, then," she adds.

A surprised look crosses her face, "Help us with what?"

Dr. Logan goes on to explain. "Some problems start before birth or within the first two years of life, and it's only by knowing Carl's history that we can help him untangle the puzzles in his head and in his emotions."

Confused, Annika asks quickly, "What makes you think Carl needs help?" She then hesitates before confessing, "I'm the one with the problem. At least that's what everyone tells me."

Dr. Logan answers, "I have a gut feeling about these things. Plus that, do you honestly think he's totally innocent?"

Annika shrugs her shoulders, leans back and shrinks deeper into the couch. Sadly she says, "I don't know what to think any more."

While the pair talks, Annika begins to feel amazingly lighter, and their easy give and take surprises her. She wonders what relief from all the feelings she's been carrying around would feel like. Or if, in fact, she would ever get any relief at all.

The therapist looks at her watch indicating that their time is up and Annika, not wanting to put anyone out, nearly jumps up to leave.

The troubled mom confides, "I haven't felt close to anyone in ages. Somehow I think I've been missing in action."

With a knowing smile Elizabeth guesses, "Like you've walked away from yourself?"

She agrees and acknowledges, "It was more like I ran away from myself. Walking would have been too slow of a process to describe what has been happening to me."

Giving reassurances, Elizabeth says, "Finding your way back is a process. You're strong. You'll make it."

Annika tries to interpret, "You really mean I'm a puddle. Right?"

The therapist's wisdom shows, "It takes more courage to cry than to clam up."

Elizabeth's comment is a mystery to Annika, but she decides to leave it alone and just stick with the process Dr. Logan offers her right now. She's beginning to discover that she can handle assistance but only in one small dose at a time.

38

Rose walks with purpose into the waiting room at the Children and Family Services Offices and sees Annika waiting impatiently for her. Rose takes her cue from the tension Annika emanates so simply gestures for her to follow her into a cramped, picture-lined office. As soon as they clear the doorway, the social worker closes the door behind them.

Annika can barely wait until they're alone and words burst from her, "You have destroyed my family!"

Taken aback, the case worker says, "I beg your pardon?"

Challenging her, Annika cries, "You have single-handedly wrecked my peaceful home."

Rose retorts trying to contain her own anger. "Mrs. Williams, I haven't done anything to you or your family."

Annika hisses, "That's a lie!"

The usually calm social worker sits hard in her chair. With shock-filled eyes, she is confused and hurt by Annika's words. With great difficulty Rose invites her, "Please, let's sit down and talk about this calmly."

Displaying a side Rose has never seen before, the irate mom shouts, "I don't want to sit! I'm furious!"

"Because...?" Rose prompts.

"Because you put Carl in my home without telling us about his history."

Rose finally grasps the situation and lets out a low whistle under her breath. "That's what this is all about?"

Annika glares at her, puts her hands on her hips and waits for an explanation.

Rose continues, "And you feel like I tricked you?"

"Exactly!" Annika exclaims, "You duped us into taking a very damaged child."

Trying to remain within her professional role, she explains, "There was only limited information available before Carl was placed with you. We have guidelines..."

Again, shouting one octave below the top of her voice Annika says, "I don't buy it!"

"What's he done?" Rose wonders aloud.

Annika answers as best she can, "He's so sneaky and deceptive I don't know yet."

The normally caring social worker responds in an offhanded manner that's uncharacteristic of her, "Well, at least he didn't kill anyone."

Breathless, the mother asks, "Is that a possibility?" Stunned, she falls into a chair, wringing her hands and rubbing her face.

The social worker is silent while she writes an address on a paper then hands it to Annika. "Go back and see Joe in 'Archives.' He'll show you what they have of Carl's records."

Aghast, Annika asks, "You mean they're available now?"

Full of sorrow, Rose nods, "I hope it's not too late. Maybe by knowing his past, he can have a future."

∼

Annika walks quickly to the front door of the State Office Building. She is intense and nervous and much too fearful to have hope that this trip will be useful at all.

As she enters the building, Joe somberly meets her at the information desk. He takes her down a dark messy hall, a frequently used passage to a dozen offices with doors posed in a variety of positions, some open, some closed and others barely ajar.

At the end of the hall Joe opens a door to a large, bare room with chipped gray walls. He holds the door open and motions for Annika to enter.

The old man gestures toward the long table in the center of the room that's covered with several, large brown accordion file folders. The man finally speaks. "There you are."

Incredulous, Annika asks, "Which are his?"

"All of them," he retorts drolly.

She gasps and can barely get her words past her tense lips. "All of these belong to Carl?"

Joe nods, almost embarrassed, then backs out closing the door as he exits the room. Annika stands glued to the floor with her eyes fixed on the bulging folders.

She finally takes several deep cleansing-like breaths as she approaches the table with unexplained caution. Prepared to take notes, Annika pulls a small spiral notebook and pen out of her handbag and sinks into the chair.

The old clock hanging high on the dingy wall reads 4:30. It seems to her that she'd just arrived so is stunned to realize she's been there for a few hours. Although she's read half the files, she is still increasingly shocked over what is written on the pages before her. Sadly, she dabs at the leakage from her eyes then throws another used tissue in the waste can.

Stunned, Annika suddenly realizes the room she occupies has grown dark so she locates the light switch and flips the lights on. Even in the low-watt light it's obvious that her eyes are sunken and her usual carefully applied makeup is smeared from her tears. She periodically paces around the room.

Gnawing at the energy bar she fishes from her bag, Annika continues writing in her notebook. The clock now reads 8 p.m. and she's surrounded by a deafening silence that comes from the rest of the building.

Suddenly Annika cannot make herself read one more detail about Carl's life. Although she's never felt close to Carl, she is completely startled to discover that what she's found in his records thoroughly disturbs her.

At first tears trickle down her face, but then they begin gushing from her eyes. Determined to do something, Annika blindly stumbles to the bathroom down the dark hall and collapses in front of the toilet. No matter how hard she tries or wants to quit, Annika cannot stop sobbing and begins vomiting profusely.

Eventually she pulls herself together to some degree, collects her things in that awful office, and runs from the dark, empty building. For no reason known to her, she hides her face in shame as she flees into the night.

39

Lexi kneels on a chair pulled out from the Williams' kitchen table and deals boldly colored playing cards to the boys. Jarren and Carl sit across the table from each other and make faces showing displeasure when they receive cards they don't like. They all keep a nervous eye on the kitchen door.

Finished dealing, Lexi flops around in the chair and collects her cards. "Dealer's choice," she says. "Five card draw, deuces wild."

Both boys roll their eyes at the girly-sounding game and rearrange the cards in their hands. Lexi is ready to give them new cards.

Jarren says, "Gimme three."

Lexi asks, "Carl?"

Carl surveys his cards then states, "None for me."

The trio antes up with pennies as they make their way around the table.

Lexi speaks in hushed tones, "Daddy would skin us if he knew what we were doing."

Carl reacts, "What's wrong with this?"

Jarren and Lexi look at each other sheepishly and giggle. Lexi responds firmly, "We're Baptist, geek."

Carl makes an ugly face at Lexi. As they continue playing, Jarren sees Carl slip a card from the bottom of the deck and growls at his brother, "Put that back, Carl!"

The young boy looks directly at Jarren and smiles his sly smile. "What do you mean?" he asks innocently.

Jarren takes on a fatherly tone with him. "Cheating isn't okay around here."

"And neither is playing poker," Carl snarles.

Jarren glares at him.

Carl's voice get louder as he nervously handles his cards. The younger boy shouts, "You're always right, aren't you, Jarren?"

Lexi butts in and speaks in her stage whisper that usually makes them laugh, but not this time. "He's not always right," she says full of conviction, "but if he says you cheated, you cheated! Put it back, Carl!"

In response, Carl stands up, tears his cards up then throws them across the room. Carl hisses, "You're picking on me just like everyone else does. Go shit in your hats!"

Jarren collects himself and stands to defend his turf if necessary. Lexi hears Annika in the next room and hurriedly collects the cards.

Lexi then calls to her mother as Carl slinks away from the situation and out the back door. "Mama, Carl's swearing."

⤞ *40* ⤝

Annika is disheveled and lays in a half reclined position on the couch in Elizabeth's office. Elizabeth sits quietly on a chair near her. They both wait silently with the only source of noise in the room being the ornate clock that sits comfortably on the mantle of the old fashioned fireplace nearby.

When she's ready, Annika curls up in a fetal position and sobs like she'll never stop. Elizabeth waits attentively until until the grieving woman's weeping subsides.

The psychologist speaks softly, "Where are the tears for you?"

"For me?" she blinks.

Elizabeth persists. "Annika, you cry for Lady and your family. You even weep for Carl. When will you cry for yourself?" Annika bristles, "I don't like self-pity!"

The therapist counters, "You think it's self pity that drives you to tears?"

Annika asks, "What else would it be?"

Elizabeth encourages her, "You tell me."

Annika looks at the therapist out of the corner of her eye, not sure where Elizabeth is going with her tough questions, but has nothing to say at this moment.

"There is a difference between liking someone and loving them," the therapist instructs. "Are you disappointed in your family?"

Annika nods vigorously and her eyes glisten with tears. "I got depressed and was disappearing right in front of their eyes and they didn't do anything to help. Not one of them."

Elizabeth's gestures indicate to Annika that the therapist understands her situation and feelings well. She clarifies for her client. "They couldn't help you, Annika. They didn't understand what was happening to you and they still don't."

Annika's reaction to Elizabeth's comments is intense. "When will they get it?" she wonders aloud.

The mature woman shrugs her shoulders ever so slightly, "Maybe later. Maybe never."

The hopeful look on Annika's face fades rapidly, sadly leaving her with more questions than answers.

⤳ *41* ⤳

The previously contented mother is in her garden, a site of great happiness in the past. She's on her knees cutting away the dead flowers from their stalks. As she slowly moves down the rows of her precious flowers, she loosens the dirt at their base and adds fresh peat moss around their roots.

Annika hears her name called. Annika looks up, frowns and waves lamely to her neighbor Lee as she leans against the back fence.

Lee looks like she's up for a good chat. "I haven't seen you out here lately like I usually do."

Annika's expression and voice are dull and lifeless, "Been busy."

Lee wants more information so goes after it, "You don't look good to me. Are you sick?"

Annika shrugs but remains careful and simply says, "No. Life struck."

"Want to tell me about it?" Lee persists.

"No, not now," the unhappy mother says.

Lee nods quickly and comments sarcastically, "Yeah, maybe sometime when you're not being so stubborn."

A wave of concern washes over the neighbor's face, but she knows Annika well enough to know not to push and heads back home without another word.

Frustrated with Lee, Annika digs furiously and catches a reflection of the sun off a metal object in the dirt. She reaches into the back of the flowerbed to collect the metal and suddenly moans in pain. She immediately yanks her hand back. She's bleeding.

This time she searches more carefully by parting the growth and examining the area visually. Shocked, she finds Zeb's old slaughterhouse knife that's been missing from her kitchen drawer. The long, thin, filet-like blade is spotted with her blood now. But Annika thinks she sees something more on the blade that just her own fresh blood.

⚘ *42* ⚘

Like many lazy summer afternoons Zeb leans under the hood of this car and makes some adjustments on the engine. In the past she's always loved watching him tinker around, hands greasy and clothes comfortably messy.

But today she's on a different emotional plane, and he's concentrating so hard he doesn't hear Annika come into the garage. He startles when she suddenly appears next to the car.

"There you are," he says with pleasure in his voice. "I couldn't find you earlier." In spite of her physical nearness she looks sort of preoccupied to him. "Are you okay?" he queries.

Annika shakes her head then struggles to muster the courage to speak her mind. She finally is ready and says, "You've never been dishonest before. Why now, Zeb?"

He sees how serious his wife is and immediately defends himself. "I've never lied to you, Annika."

She persists. "You withheld the truth. That's not honesty."

Instinctively he knows now is no time to play around as he wipes his nervous hands on a grimy towel. He frowns his concern. "I wish I knew what you're talking about."

She means business and he knows it. "You didn't tell me about Carl's past," she charges.

"What about his past?" Zeb wants to know.

Annika leans into Zeb and stops just short of being right in his face. She's so close, in fact, that he can smell her angry breath.

She goes on the attack. "That he was neglected by his mother and left with no food or water in a motel room for three days while she 'went out.'"

He's shocked into silence.

Words long buried fly out of her mouth. "And he was sexually abused by his mother's boyfriend and then by a foster mom."

Zeb sinks sadly to the floor but Annika's anger gives her strength. She's hot and goes after it. "And if that's not enough, he had his leg broken by one of his eight foster fathers."

Tears leap from Zeb's eyes. "Merciful God," he cries.

"And that's just a start," she says collecting steam. "Shall I go on?"

Zeb shakes his head and signals for her to halt. He takes a few rugged breaths and pleads with her. "I didn't know all that, Baby."

She is still angry. "Maybe not, but you also didn't bother to tell me what you did know."

Annika stands her ground with hands on both hips. She looks defiant and resigned. "You bruised my heart, Zebediah."

Zeb covers his face with his hands as Annika disappears into the house.

~

Ready for bed already, Lexi sits on her bed with her head hung low as she reads their local paper. She picks up the cell phone that lays next to her and listens silently for a few moments. She then closes the phone and wipes her eyes.

Annika walks by her daughter's open door and sees Lexi looking distraught. The mother walks to the bed and reads the headline over Lexi's shoulder: "Two Teen Girls Stabbed: Slasher on the Loose."

"Oh, Mama," Lexi cries, "this is so awful!"

Annika sits on the bed, takes her daughter into her arms and rocks her as the teenage girl sobs.

⮰ *43* ⮰

Annika nervously enters the children's unit of their county psychiatric hospital, the Willow Rehabilitation Hospital, and finds Elizabeth inside talking with Nurse Bob, the head nurse. She sheepishly approaches the therapist with her face full of questions.

Elizabeth reaches her hand out to touch Annika's shoulder and says, "I'm glad you came. I want you to see some of these children."

Annika cringes and quietly asks, "What for?"

The psychologist almost brushes off Annika's concerns with a flippant, "You'll see. Come along."

Dr. Elizabeth Logan leads Annika down one side of a long therapeutic looking room. Heavy wooden doors line the outside walls all around the unit with observation windows cut out of the walls beside each door. A crowded nurses' station is located in the middle of the room.

Several staff members dressed in street clothes mill around the area under the benevolent yet watchful eye of Nurse Bob and most have a child in tow. A few of the rooms marked with "Quiet Room" are occupied by wild-eyed looking children who are being observed by note taking staff sitting outside the observation windows. Since it's visiting hours, several parents are also nearby, watching how the professionals handle their children.

Elizabeth talks as she walks. "Maybe," she says with some mystery in her voice, "you'll see someone you recognize."

Seeing the unit has not yet cleared up any questions for her, in fact, just the opposite. Annika is still puzzled.

The pair stops and looks through a window where a young girl is huddled like an injured animal in the corner of the room. The staff at the window explains to Billie's parents, Tonya and Max, that ten-year-old Billie is all scruffy from her efforts to control everyone and the situation and is having an especially bad day.

Unimpressed by her parents presence, Billie hurls obscenities at the staff there to redirect her, "I'm gonna kill you!" The girl graphically describes her plans shouting, "I'll slit your fucking throat then spit down your neck hole," while her parents are horrified.

Billie's face is normally beautiful but is now contorted with rage. She spits at them and a big glob of saliva lands on the observation glass with a thud. Surprised, Annika jumps back from the glass.

Not finished yet, she yells more, "Then I'll go kick your mother's ass."

The psychologist explains to Annika and the parents, "Pretty graphic, huh? She wants to be in charge, but can't be."

"Why is she so, uh, nasty?," Tonya asks of the therapist.

"She's really terrified," she explains, "but turns her feelings into anger instead."

Max shudders and says, "No one could cuddle up to that."

"Exactly," replies Elizabeth.

"Exactly?" quizzes Annika.

Elizabeth smiles a knowing smile then moves to the next door. Unsure, Annika follows along anyway and sees a little girl talking to a nurse who is sitting at eye level with seven-year-old Emma.

Dr. Logan introduces Annika to Emma's parents and explains what's going on and encourages Annika to watch the exchange between the girl and the nurse carefully.

Nurse Dina, a calm, mature woman, holds her hand under Emma's chin. "Sweetie," she says with a syrupy voice, "look at me. Look right into my eyes when you speak to me."

Emma starts to roll her eyes then reluctantly complies and Dina continues, "Good job. Now what do you need?"

Emma pipes in, "May I go to the bathroom?"

Dina nods, smiles at her while maintaining eye contact, stands up, takes the little girl by the hand, and they walk toward the bathroom together. Emma's parents don't quite get what's going on but are happy their daughter is being cooperative.

Annika and Elizabeth wander further down the unit and past the kitchen where Annika notices a lock on the refrigerator and cupboard doors. Annika puts her hand on the therapist's arm to stop her and nods toward the kitchen. Barely able to conceal her anxiety, Annika worries over the sight of the locks.

Elizabeth guesses the mother's concern and asks, "That looks mean, doesn't it?" Then she goes on to explain. "Kids who have been starved often hoard food to be eaten later and don't know if or when they are full. We have to help them regulate their appetites."

A look of recognition flashes across Mrs. Williams' face when she remembers their first picnic with Carl. She recalls his plate piled high with food and talking to Zeb later that evening about he boy's voracious appetite. So maybe that's what was going on, she thinks.

Annika reports one of her observations to see if that is what Elizabeth means. She says, "I've found cookie wrappers in my cupboard that are puffed up and closed tight but the cookies are missing."

With parents still observing, Dina and Emma go to one of the many workstations to begin another project. Other staff members mill around tending to other children in the milieu.

Elizabeth flashes a knowing smile while Annika waves her hand in Emma's direction. A look of guilt crosses her face before she haltingly speaks. "And about that eye contact thing – when Carl looks directly at me I think he's lying."

The psychologist simply comments, "I know."

Annika questions her immediately. "How do you know? You've never met him."

"Kids who are traumatized in their early years," Elizabeth informs, "exhibit similar behaviors. Those behaviors are the symptoms of the problem."

Annika is puzzled.

Elizabeth continues, "And one way we diagnose these kids is to look at those behaviors and get to know their mothers."

"Huh?" the mother says blinking in amazement.

Dr. Logan probes, "Are you mad at Carl?"

"Well, yes, a little," Annika admits, "but I hate to admit that."

Elizabeth pushes, "I mean really mad! Madder than you've ever been at Jarren or Lexi?"

She hangs her head and Annika says solemnly, "I'm afraid so."

The psychologist goes on to explain, "Reactive Attachment Disorder is the only mental illness where mothers are royally pissed at their children."

Now Annika is totally lost.

"With other problems," Elizabeth continues, "moms are sad or worried or sorry, but not totally angry like the mothers of these children."

A small light goes on her her brain as Annika says, "That's the problem? He has Reactive Attachment Disorder?" The woman sees how the term comes off her tongue and lets the idea sink in.

Elizabeth nods and Annika wants to debate, "But he's not exactly like these kids," she says somewhat challengingly.

The therapist clarifies, "The disorder comes in degrees and we don't know how sick or disturbed that initial bond with his biological mother was yet."

They're distracted by yelling from across the unit. The two turn to watch an exchange between nurse Kim and her young charge who's starting to losing control.

James screeches at the top of his lungs, "I don't wanna go to my room!"

Kim remains calm. Her eye contact, like her voice remains soft, steady and firm. "Just for a ten minute time-out, James. You're having trouble with directions now, so I want you to go and think about your choices."

Annika notices that a sad woman who might be the boy's mother, Georgia, sits off to the side watching.

James insists, "No! I won't go! You're not my boss."

The angrier James becomes, the sappier Kim gets. Her voice is full of syrup. "I know this is gonna shock you, Sweetie, but I am your boss for today. I see you don't want to leave my side. How wonderful!"

The little boy challenges, "That's not wonderful!"

Kim retorts, "Sure it is, Darling. I don't want you to be away from me either, so instead I'll accept ten minutes of strong sitting."

Kim maintains kind eye contact and is calm while James glares at her. Kim walks to a place along the wall and points to where she wants him to sit.

James shouts, "I ain't sitting!"

Kim remains firm, "I'm the boss and I want you to follow directions."

Bob, the nurse manager, walks to Kim's side and watches the exchange with some amusement on his face. Kim speaks to Bob but knows James is listening and explains with some drama in her voice, "Goodness! James doesn't think he has to mind me. Can you imagine that?" she says with a lot of phony in her voice.

James screams at Kim, "Go fuck yourself!" while James' mother looks like she might swallow her tongue.

Kim blandly replies, "Not yet, Sweetheart, but maybe I'll think about it after you sit for me."

Nurse Bob speaks to Kim in a pronounced stage whisper, "You know, Kim, I don't think James knows how to sit. I think he's much too young."

The boy becomes even more furious, "Screw you too, Bob. I ain't too young!"

Kim sticks with her challenge. "Maybe so, Bob. But I think he's too weak to sit for ten minutes."

James totally resents the implication and yells, "You're full of shit, Kim. I'm strong and you know it!"

The nurse has a twinkle in her eyes and a "gotcha" tone in her voice. "Prove it," she challenges, while sending a half smile to the boy's mother.

Believing the gauntlet has been thrown down, James stops a moment and glares hard at Kim as he considers his options. After several seconds he storms over to the site

Kim had pointed out and flops down facing the wall with his hands and legs folded as requested.

Kim coos, "Good choice, Sweetie. Time has started and maybe you are strong enough. We'll see for sure this time."

Kim turns away from James and flashes the mother and Nurse Bob a wicked "I won" gesture as Bob and Kim give each other a sneaky high five.

Elizabeth finds the exchange between the two professionals entertaining and she smiles, but Annika frowns as she watches.

"What was that all about?" Annika asks.

The psychologist explains, "These kids don't trust anyone so they go for total control and won't follow even the most simple suggestions. But here's the rub, they can't and shouldn't have control at all over much, especially over others, because they are children."

Mrs. Williams tries to understand. "They act naughty so they can be in control of everyone and every situation?"

"Right," Elizabeth responds to the mothers. "The staff is using several good techniques to try earn his cooperation."

Georgia states, "They remained so calm. I could never do that."

Elizabeth says, "That's very important and part of helping them. But you're right, it is very hard to do. They're such strong little individuals."

At the appointed time Kim relieves James of his sitting position, gives the boy a warm hug, and then they go on to the next activity.

Annika sees the obvious difference in James' behaviors, is fascinated, so pays attention to all the activity around her.

As the pair walks toward the door, Dr. Logan waves toward the unit and says, "These children are receiving treatment for their attachment difficulties. Did you notice how the staff uses a tag-team approach?"

Annika nods and shares, "Not once have I gotten Carl to do what he didn't want to do."

Elizabeth pats Annika's shoulder and gives her the kindest of smiles. As they exit, the psychologist pauses at the door to point out a notice to Annika, one hanging on the bulletin board. Annika reads it and makes a mental note.

"ANNOUNCEMENT!!"

"Please join parents of children with RAD.

Share your experiences and learn what can be done to help your youngsters.

Dr. Elizabeth Logan will be available for guidance."

☞ *44* ☜

An unmarked dark sedan drives up, and the driver parks at the curb in front of a home in a lovely tree-lined suburban neighborhood. The men inside the car talk quietly for a few moments before they leave the car in unison and walk up the sidewalk to a lovely well-manicured home.

It would be easy to guess when looking at the tidy, suit wearing pair with neat short haircuts that they're either insurance guys without their brief cases or plainclothes police officers.

It is the middle of the afternoon when the doorbell rings at the Williams' home. Annika crosses the living room and looks out the window near the front door and sees two men she's never met. She instantly becomes anxious, which surprises and puzzles her, but Annika opens the door anyway.

The two immediately hold their badges up for her inspection and introduce themselves as Police Officers Sullivan and Newell. She examines their badges carefully then invites them into the living room.

As the duo enters her home, Annika is overwhelmed with feelings she can't readily identify so she fidgets with her clothing as they talk to her.

Officer Sullivan explains in a kind, soft voice, "We're investigating the stabbings of two young girls from this area of town."

Sadly she nearly gasps, "How terrible for their families."

The officer nods and persists, "The girls live nearby. Have any of your children attended Lincoln Junior High? Or, do you know any of the students who attend that school?"

Nervously, the mother reports, "My daughter starts eighth grade there soon. She knows who the girls are, but that's all."

The look on Officer Newell's face indicates he finds that fact worth noting.

Annika talks a little too fast, but continues, "My youngest will be in sixth grade at Bristol elementary, but I don't know his friends yet."

The pair doesn't grasp their family arrangement yet, so both look at her with a puzzled expression. Sullivan frowns and says, "I beg your pardon?"

Annika thinks this is really none of their business, but nonetheless, she reluctantly describes their family constellation. "Carl, my youngest, was recently adopted."

The officers begin to get it. Officer Newell hands her his business card as Annika walks them to the door where she finds herself impatiently waiting for them to leave.

Newell concludes, "Call us if your kids should mention either girl or if you notice anything unusual."

She nods and closes the door behind them. Feeling more nervous for some reason, Annika leans against the door and shudders.

∾

Still restless after the visit from Officers Sullivan and Newell earlier that day, Annika finds she sorely needs to take a few moments out of her busy day to shake off the disturbing feelings left over from the encounter.

She sits quietly at the dressing table in their bedroom. As Annika writes in her journal, her hand flies as if separate from her body and her brows knit over her eyes intensely focused on the page before her. In fact, the mother is so engrossed in her task that she doesn't notice her daughter silently pacing the hall outside the bedroom door.

After several laps back and forth, trips that were unsuccessful in gaining her mother's attention, the girl finally stops at Annika's door and lingers a moment before she speaks. With hesitation, Lexi says, "You're busy..."

Annika looks up expectantly at her daughter and answers, "A little, but what is it, Dear?"

The teen is nervous and stammers which startles Annika because this behavior is out of character for her daughter. Lexi's usual nature is relaxed and easy going.

Lexi says slowly, "I need to tell you something."

Suddenly concerned, Annika gets up from the table and walks over to Lexi with worry on her face. She puts her arms around Lexi's shoulders, leads her to the bed and sits down on the edge of the bed with her.

Anxious, the girl gestures toward the door indicating it should be closed while she is talking to her mother.

Annika senses immediacy and crosses the room and closes the door tightly, then returns to her daughter's side. Annika can feel Lexi begin to tremble.

Her mother whispers, "Please, Sweetheart..."

Lexi's face is screwed up with worry, "You want us to tell you stuff, even if it's really bad. Right?"

Thoughtfully, Annika agrees.

Lexi stammers, "This is about Carl. Well, and about me, too."

"Okay..." the mother responds.

She reluctantly goes on. "One day when Carl and I were here alone he tried to mess with me."

Guarding her reactions, Annika asks, "Mess with you, how?"

Looking terrified, the girls shakes more. "When I got out of the shower, I didn't know he was in the bathroom."

Annika is instantly furious but carefully modulates her voice so Lexi isn't frightened by her reaction. "Do you mean he came in the bathroom when you were there?" She pauses but can't help but ask her distraught daughter, "Were you hurt?"

The young girl bursts out crying and looks totally embarrassed at the same time.

Lexi shakes her head vigorously, but fesses up. "He tried, but I didn't let him."

Filled with fear, Annika asks cautiously, "What did you do?"

With power in her voice and nearly shouting, Lexi answers, "I told him,'Get out!' Then I kicked him between his legs as hard as I could." The youngster is flooded with relief but still thinks she's done something wrong. "I'm so sorry, Mama," she says as she weeps harder.

As she engulfs her daughter in a bold embrace, Annika shakes her head and states clearly, "I'm glad you did that."

Lexi blinks in disbelief, "You are?"

While continuing to console her, the mother shares, "I'm mad about what happened to you. It's not okay for anyone to try to hurt you."

The girl, still completely distraught, collapses into her mother, who consoles her sobbing daughter. After a few minutes of hearing only the sounds of broken hearts, Annika speaks softly, "I'm so glad you weren't hurt, Lexi, but I just need to ask. Why didn't you tell me before?"

Lexi's sobs turn to wailing when she is finally able to catch her breath. She spits out, "Because he said he'd kill me if I told on him."

Annika Williams' fists clench and her jaw tightens precariously while she glares at nothing in particular.

⤟ *45* ⤠

The fierce mother is determined like never before as she half stomps, half sneaks her way up the stairs to the second floor wearing some of her rattiest gardening clothes.

With long strides Annika arrives at the appointed door and pays no attention to the "PRIVATE: KEEP OUT!!" sign that hangs at eye level on Carl's door. With a solid push she practically bursts into the room.

Prepared this time, she wears rubber gloves and holds a long necked fork, the kind that she and Zeb use when they barbecue chicken and steaks on the grill. Unsure of what she's looking for after Annika's last experience with Carl's room, she at least has a good idea where to look.

With a newfound resolve on her face the sturdy woman walks directly to Carl's bed, and with significant force lifts the mattress to expose a new mess that has developed there in his hiding place. Annika uses the long tool and her gloved hands to sift through the obnoxious mound of junky items Carl has stored beneath his sleeping place.

The wasted and moldy food smells nauseate her and make her gag, but, more determined than ever, Annika holds her breath and leans in for a closer look anyway. Before long her face clouds up as she reaches deep into the refuse pile for a specific item. She feels sad that the place she'd hoped would be a place of comfort for her new son looks like this.

Slowly, Annika lifts a pearl bracelet from the rubble and, for some unknown reason, clutches it to her chest as if she were hanging on to it for dear life itself.

⤳ 46 ⤳

It's late in the evening and the Williams brood have gone to bed, so the house is silent, a situation that's pretty rare with their lively family. Only Zeb and Annika are up and involved in their own quiet, relaxing activities.

Zeb walks into the kitchen and grabs a cup from the cupboard for coffee from the ever-warm pot on the stove. Annika is busy potting a new geranium in the kitchen sink. She's so lost in thought that this time she doesn't mind the mess she's making as she usually does.

He thinks Annika's expression looks somewhat tense even though she's doing something he knows she loves. With their recent difficulties in mind, Zeb wonders what's in store for him, especially since it looks like his beloved bride is ignoring his presence. To give her the space she seems to crave these days, he pulls a chair out from the table and sits down to read. Then he waits to see if anything comes of their closeness.

Finally Annika speaks to him but keeps her back to him and faces the kitchen sink and her planting project. Somewhat absorbed in his paper, at first Zeb wasn't sure who she is talking to.

Annika begins, "I've been thinking about my life – well, about ours really – for the past several weeks."

Zeb's breath catches in his throat and for the first time that he can remember, he is afraid to speak.

She continues, "There have been lots of changes around here and I haven't been very happy about any of them."

He risks it, "For instance?"

Annika shares softly, "I've had lots of loss. Some are obvious, some aren't. Lady for one."

Zeb agrees, "That was really sad."

She barely gives him space to comment and keeps talking, "The number of accidents around here is a big change, too."

Not realizing how it sounds, Zeb shares, "I haven't noticed."

"And the loss of our communication," she says making her point. "Apparently that's one more thing you haven't noticed."

He starts to interrupt and defend himself, but Annika shushes him and begins gathering strength. "You always ask for examples but then interrupt my answer. Do you want to hear this or not?"

Speaking honestly with his throat full of fear Zeb says, "I'm not so sure, but go on."

Her face looks older than usual as she continues, "The loss of my mental health. For the first time in my life I think I'm losing my mind."

As the driven woman talks, she ticks off items on her fingers and gets angrier and angrier as she talks. "Jarren and Lexi stay away from home more, which I understand, but," Annika adds, "I don't like it one bit."

Zeb keeps his eyes glued on her face and hopes the depth of his sadness doesn't show as he asks, "Why do they?"

For the first time Annika looks at the man who's become a stranger to her and says, "You're a wonder." She shakes her head, "For one thing, Lexi isn't safe in our home. You figure it out!"

The normally self-assured man is stunned and fights to keep his thinking from going in the direction Annika is trying to take him. He gasps and then finally stammers, "Carl hurt Lexi?"

Annika gives him the frostiest look she can muster, nods and has no words to say.

"I don't believe you!" he nearly shouts.

Annika gains steam, "It doesn't matter what you believe any more, Zeb. You left us the moment Carl walked in the front door." She hesitates a second to catch her breath. "You're so blinded by your desire to help other people's children you can't see what's happening to your own."

Zeb responds with angst in his voice, "No fair, Annika, I've been called."

"Not every child is salvageable," she retorts. Starting to tear up now, Annika points out reality. "You can't save them all."

Bereft, the minister responds, "But I can't give up on him."

Thoughtfully, Annika says, "Then you're trading us off for Carl."

He slumps against the counter and looks totally dejected while Annika collects herself and summons the internal courage to go on.

She says slowly, "I don't want you to choose between us now, but I don't want to live with you while you decide."

Stunned, Zeb asks, "What are you saying?"

"I can't get my old self back under these conditions," Annika explains clearly. "You take Carl and see what you can do with him."

"You mean Carl and I need to leave our home?" he sputters. Annika levels her gaze directly at him leaving little doubt about what she means.

Zeb is shocked. "When?"

All of Annika's emotions are bubbling to the top, but she speaks with resolve, "Now."

Tears stream down the man's contorted face and he slumps over the counter full of sorrow. Zeb fights to collect himself as he slowly leaves the kitchen, but moments later he suddenly bursts back into the room. Annika has her back to him while working with the plant. She turns part way to look at him out of the corner of her eye in an effort to keep her distress veiled, hidden from her husband.

Pleading, Zeb takes another tack and demands, "It doesn't have to be this way."

The tired woman responds firmly and with total resolve, "Yes, it does."

☞ *47* ☜

Annika drives across town with both determination and dread on her face. She begins to turn into the parking lot at the police substation, but passes the driveway at the last minute and continues to drive around the block.

Instead of driving around the block as she'd intended, she finds herself all over town while she fights a mental battle with herself. Frowning in deep thought, she nervously gnaws at her nails.

Finally, when she feels ready, Annika returns to the police station, drives into their lot and parks the car. As if walking to her death, she walks slowly into the noisy station and into a room filled with desks and ringing phones. The noise from impromptu groups of two or three officers clatters to no particular rhythm.

The timid-looking woman feels totally intimidated as she approaches a seasoned looking officer with 'Smith' beneath his badge on his chest and sits near the door under the 'Information Desk' sign.

Officer Smith sees her and asks, "What can I do for you?"

With knees knocking she speaks so softly he can barely hear her. "I'd like to talk to Officer Sullivan or Officer Newell. I'm Annika Williams."

The officer leans in to hear her better and asks, "Are they expecting you?"

Annika shakes her head deliberately and looks nearly despondent.

Smith instructs, "Have a seat and I'll see if either one is here."

Annika follows his directions and sits tentatively on the edge of her chair. After several minutes of waiting she stands and starts to edge her way toward the door. Office Newell suddenly appears before her and nods her way.

"Mrs. Williams," he says, "please come in and talk to me."

The young looking officer ushers her to an unoccupied office in the back of the room. There is a window overlooking the large communal office. She clutches her purse like a little old lady might and sits in the chair near the desk.

Annika barely squeaks out her words. "I shouldn't even be here."

"No problem," Newell says in a soothing manner. "How can I help?"

She can't stop stammering as she selects her words carefully. "You said I could call you, but I'd rather talk to you in person. And here."

Newell maintains his professionalism. "Whatever is best for you."

Sounding confused, Annika speaks deliberately, "I don't know anything, really."

Intrigued, the officer states, "Okay."

Rushing, lest she lose her nerve, Annika continues, "I've never been here before, so don't know what to do."

Helping her as best he can, Newell says, "This might be nerve wracking for you, but just take your time."

Annika takes some deep breaths before she speaks again. Then, "I found some things but I don't know if they are important."

The officer listens to her intently.

"It's just some old stuff, I think," the woman adds.

Newell coaxes her. "I'd like to see them if you'll show me."

Annika's hands shake as she removes a small cloth sack from her purse. She handles the parcel carefully as she lays it on his desk.

So he doesn't frighten his conflicted guest, Officer Newell moves slowly while he opens the sack and cautiously unfolds the towel inside. When he sees the pearl bracelet, a locket, and a large filet-like knife, he whistles under his breath.

Obviously interested, Newell asks carefully, "How did you come by these, Mrs. Williams?"

Filled with fears, but knowing she needs to come clean, she answers, "The knife is one my husband got years ago. We usually keep it in a particular drawer in the kitchen, but I noticed it was missing several weeks ago."

"Apparently it showed up," he says half to himself.

She continues, "I love to garden and I found it in the back of my flowerbed. It's still pretty sharp. I cut my finger on it when I picked it up."

Without picking up the knife the officer visually examines the blade. Questions wash over his face.

Annika points to the blade and says, "Some of the blood is mine. At first it looked like something else was on it, too, but I don't see it now."

She reaches for the knife but Newell stops her by blocking her hand with his. "I forgot," she apologizes, "I handled those things before I brought them in."

Newell nods his head, "You're not used to collecting evidence. And the locket and bracelet, where did they come from?"

Her eyes glaze over with tears and she can barely speak. She gets up, walks to the window and stands quietly looking over the bay of blue uniforms.

Unexpectedly, Annika opens the door and charges from the office leaving her purse behind. Having taken many of the officers by surprise, most watch her flee with Officer Newell close on her heels.

The panting officer shouts, "Stop her!"

As Annika nears the front door, the old Officer Smith steps in front of her and blocks her path. "Where's the sale?" he asks with a twinkle in his eyes.

"You can't hold me!" she shouts breathlessly.

Newell catches up with her and approaches her gingerly. "Easy or hard, Mrs. Williams. Your choice. I could subpoena you if you don't want to do this the easy way."

Annika shamefully hides her face. She doesn't want to cooperate, and her feet feel like they've been planted in clay.

Smith still prods her. "Mrs. Williams, you came to us. Was Officer Newell being mean to you?"

Annika ignores Smith because she's too keyed up to enjoy his particular brand of humor. "We might be talking about my child," she pleads, wishing it weren't so. "I can't do this."

Newell guides her, "Telling the truth is another way of loving someone. You want your son to be accountable for his behaviors, don't you?"

"I can't make that happen," she says convinced that's the truth.

"Yes you can. Right now," he explains.

The officer places his hand on her arm and gently guides her back to his office. She refuses to sit and stands reading the many plaques on the wall. After several minutes she speaks barely above a whisper while keeping her back to Newell.

"My son's room," she says to his amazement. "I found both bracelets in Carl's room. I don't know whose they are or how they got there."

Newell queries, "They were just lying around?"

She's reluctant to answer.

The officer suggests she take the right course of action. "This is tough, but if someone in your home is in trouble, we need to help them."

She blurts out, "They had nothing to do with this! I shouldn't have come."

Newell demonstrates his kinder side by remaining calm and giving Annika time to collect herself. Then he redirects her. "I think you wanted to tell me about the jewelry."

Annika wrestles internally before answering. The other cops near the office continue their activities but look into the office occasionally to make sure all is calm.

"I found them in his bed," she finally admits.

"In his bed?" he ponders.

She explains, "Carl came to us with only a few belongings so he hides special things for safe keeping."

Newell appears familiar of the practice and shares, "I've heard adopted and foster kids often hoard stuff with sentimental value."

She turns to him and nods, "So what happens now?"

The officer, often wise beyond his years, states, "We'll send this to the lab to see what we find. In the meantime, Mrs. Williams, go home and hug your family."

As Annika prepares to leave the room, Newell tries to console the sad woman. "Mrs. Williams," he says kindly, "You did a good thing here today."

Her entire demeanor disagrees. As she opens the door, she speaks in a voice filled with grief and guilt, "I'm a Judas."

⟿ *48* ⟾

Their new apartment is somewhat stark and sparsely furnished, a real contrast to their spacious, cozy home they had to leave at Annika's insistence. Zeb is still having a hard time justifying the move in his head.

The pair has already had a slim supper of soup and sandwiches, which would have been considered a lunch to them in their former life. Both sit in front of the television in a nearly stuporous state. Zeb is distracted by his own deep thoughts and not paying any attention to Carl who is restless and can't seem to get settled for the evening.

With an obvious agenda on his mind, Carl asks, "When are we going to move back home?"

Barely moving a muscle, Zeb responds with, "I don't know, Son."

Carl persists, "But how long do we have to be here? I want to go home."

Zeb engages mildly, "I don't know the answer to that question either. I guess we'll just have to wait and see what happens."

The boy gets up from the couch he'd been occupying and heads to the kitchen for something, although it's apparent he doesn't really know what he's looking for. After a short minute or two he comes back to stand near his father's elbow.

He has a sneer in his voice when he speaks, "I know we're here because of Annika. She's so mean."

Zeb bristles and his irritation with the boy's line of questioning is beginning to show.

Nearly shouting in frustration, he retorts, "That's not it, Carl! We just have some things to work out before we can go back home. That's all there is to it."

Unexpectedly, especially since they haven't had even one visitor in their new apartment, the doorbell rings and startles them both. Irritated, Zeb gets up and as he opens the door, Officers Newell and Sullivan present their badges.

Officer Sullivan speaks first. "May we come in?"

Zeb wonders what's going on and frowns but steps aside and lets the officers enter the living room.

In the background Carl looks like his life is passing before his eyes, and he begins to tremble. The boy can't stand the new level of discomfort so, looking guilty, leaves the room retreating to his bedroom.

Sullivan makes a silent note of the boy's departure and continues talking to Zeb. "Reverend Williams," Sullivan says calmly, "We must inform you that we have a warrant for the arrest of Carl John Williams."

Zeb is dumbfounded and stutters, "What? What in God's name for?"

Newell joins in, "We have evidence that implicates your son in the stabbing injuries of Sally Weiss and Michele Tate."

"Who?" the shocked father asks.

Newell continues, "The adolescent girls who were recently attacked in your neighborhood. We have reason to believe they were both stabbed by the same person."

"God have mercy!" Zeb exclaims, "Carl is eleven years old." He blinks hard then gathers his courage. "What evidence?"

Sullivan chimes in, "I'm afraid we aren't at liberty to share that information, Sir. The investigation is still ongoing."

"And the charges?" Zeb wonders aloud.

In his calmest, most professional voice Sullivan answers, "He'll be booked on two counts of assault with a deadly weapon. Because of the seriousness of the charges and his age, Carl will be held at the Detention Center until his court hearing."

Suddenly, a crash followed by the sound of shattering glass hitting the floor in the back of the apartment reaches their ears all the way in the living room.

Everyone acts instinctively. Newell dashes from the apartment while Officer Sullivan and Zeb rush in to Carl's bedroom. When they throw open the door to the boy's room, Carl is no where to be found. Only the window, splintered into thousands of pieces, greets them.

Sullivan quickly picks his way through the glass shards to look out the window in hopes of spotting Carl. Without a word the officer runs from the apartment and in the direction he thinks Carl and Newell might have run. Zeb is on Sullivan's heels.

Once outside, the minister and Sullivan hear the sounds of shouting and scuffling coming from around the building.

As he runs toward the noise, Zeb tries to identify sounds he's never heard before. When he catches up with Carl, he realizes the guttural sounds he could hear at a distance were actually coming from his son.

Horror stricken, Zeb feels the hair on the back of his neck stand on end. He realizes he has heard similar sounds before, but they've come from injured dogs, never from humans. And especially, never from Carl. The haunting sounds leave Zeb nearly disoriented.

Officer Newell gets to Carl before Sullivan and begins to struggle with the child whose strength far surpasses that of most boys his age. Sullivan lends a hand to forcefully apply handcuffs to the writhing youngster.

"Okay, Carl, that's enough!" Newell shouts. "Cooperate with us and this will go easier for you."

Still determined he can get free, Carl snarles, "Get your fucking hands off me! You can't do this to me. My Dad's a minister!"

Sullivan responds with fake shock, "So?"

Carl wails making the neighbors think the child was being beaten within an inch of his life. Even with Carl's weepy display Zeb notices there are no tears in the boy's eyes, and the youngster looks like he's been struck by a bus.

Carl manages a last ditch effort, "Daddy!"

Zeb's first instinct is to rescue his son from the hands of Newell and Sullivan, but his well-developed principles and conscience won't let him respond in a way that would cause the boy more harm in the long run.

Instead, Zeb pleads, "Cooperate with them, Carl. I'll see what can be done about this situation first thing in the morning."

This is not what Carl wants to hear, and he lets loose with a barrage of words that had previously been aimed at Annika. "I thought at least you loved me. Fuck you, Dad!"

Having gotten their charge under their control, the officers stuff Carl in the back seat of their unmarked patrol car and turn on the lights as they drive away.

Left standing alone in the front yard of the apartment building, it is then that the reverend notices that the neighbors have been at their windows during the entire fracas and have been taking it all in.

Zeb thinks that he can't quite recall a time in his entire life when he's felt so mortified. He returns to his apartment totally dejected.

⤜ *49* ⤛

Zeb knows that this visiting time is unusual and is determined to make the best of it. He hasn't seen Carl since he was taken to the juvenile hall several days ago and wants his son to know he'll support him through the process. Zeb's knows he's here today to deliver that message to his son.

The serious father is ushered into a small, barren office. With a generic table and two chairs in the middle of the room there's not much room for a meeting, but it'll have to do.

Zeb waits only seconds when a mature orderly brings a calm Carl into the room. The staff member says, "You only have fifteen minutes to visit," and closes the door behind him as he leaves the little room.

Carl immediately sits down and gives Zeb a huge, toothy grin.

This is a strange situation for Zeb so he feels nervous and secretly wishes this wasn't happening. Stating the obvious, Zeb says, "There's not much time to talk."

Abruptly getting right to his agenda, Carl pleads, "Daddy, please get me out of here. Take me home."

Zeb wasn't expecting to be pressured by the boy so is taken aback. "Uh, no, Son. There's still work for you to do here."

Instantly tense, Carl nearly yells, "Work? What work?"

Trying to sound calm though he doesn't feel that way, Zeb answers, "You still need time to figure out what went wrong and how to fix it."

"Wrong with me?" Carl shouts. "There's nothing wrong with me! Did Annika put you up to this?"

Zeb nonchalantly shrugs. Zeb doesn't want to discuss treatment issues with Carl, which is especially true since the boy is about to lose it. "Calm down, Carl. You just need to learn to cope with life better."

By now Carl is screaming, "Cope? Cope you say? You go to hell and let's see how you cope with that!"

Carl jumps up and rushes the door. The orderly hears the commotion and opens the door for him. Carl sneers at Zeb as he leaves the room.

Zeb sits alone, dumbfounded and wondering.

⇀ *50* ↼

Zeb stands on a corner on main street downtown among the crowds that have come out for the music festival. He impatiently fiddles with a long stemmed red rose while he waits. Suddenly he breaks into a sheepish grin as Annika walks out of the crowd toward him.

He can't help himself, "Beautiful Annika!" he croons.

In spite of all their years together her eye contact with him is fleeting and almost shy. Even though he places the rose in her hand, Annika appears somewhat disbelieving.

"Uh-huh," she says slightly sarcastically.

Trying to keep from going too fast, he says softly, "I was afraid you'd change your mind about meeting me."

"I considered it," she says, but thinks that her husband knows her entirely too well.

She feels her hands trembling slightly and jams them into her pockets so Zeb doesn't notice. Her husband is anxious, too, and suggests, "Shall we walk?"

The streets are filled with laughing, talking people who are responding to the strains of music coming from several different bands and choirs. The whole scene strikes both of them as romantic, and occasionally they stop to watch as couples dance to the music.

They amble down the busy street stopping occasionally on the sidewalk to look at the menus at the small neighborhood restaurants.

Zeb breaks the silence, "It's been such a long time since our last date."

"Another era," she muses back, "and a lifetime ago."

He wonders aloud, "Is there any chance we can just pretend it's the old days?"

Annika's fears jump into her throat. "It's not the old days, Zeb. Please go slow and let's just see what happens."

They stop at an intersection that has been blocked off for the gospel choir and watch with fascination. Zeb quietly tries to stuff down feelings that are rising to the surface.

After several moments of being lost in the music and in the moment, Zeb turns his attention back to Annika and picks up the conversation where they left off.

As they walk down the street, he responds to what seems like it just came out of the blue. "That's fair, but I don't think you like me much these days."

"Where would you get that notion?" she asks. He thinks she's being sarcastic until he sees a softness he's sorely missed come to her eyes.

Slightly surprised, he responds slowly, "How could I believe anything else?"

Annika begins to protest but with a smile in his eyes he holds his hand up to her lips to stop her. Nearby a band is playing slow, romantic music; he offers both his hands to her in a silent invitation to dance.

She hesitates a moment to consider her answer, then smiles and takes his hands as he leads her to the dance area. Annika glides into his arms and is stunned at how readily she nestles into him.

A smiling Zeb remains silent out of fear that doing anything else might break whatever spell has been cast over them tonight. Unlike his bride of so many years, Zeb is not surprised at how quickly he responds to her wrapped in his arms.

Finally, he breaks the silence. "You smell marvelous. I've missed that."

"You mean," she asks jokingly, "I smell better than my usual essence of peat moss?"

He nods and adds, "And way better than your other favorite, eau du evergreen."

Annika gets into their gentle ribbing. "And I can readily tell, Sir, that you have updated your Right Guard."

Zeb blushes. "I wanted a new image. The old one got tarnished."

They walk slowly away from the dance floor, hand-in-hand, and stroll peacefully through the throngs of people. Eventually their silence is broken by Annika this time.

Her face is serious. "I know we agreed to save discussion of the kids for another time, but I have to ask. How's Carl?"

"Okay, I guess." He hesitates, then asks carefully, "Sweetheart, can this just be our night?"

Slightly embarrassed, Annika replies, "Yes, of course. I'm sorry. I need to learn how to keep from talking about the children all the time."

Zeb listens intently while she continues.

"They've been my life for so long I wonder who I am without them," she wonders aloud.

Against their agreement and his better judgment, Zeb jumps into the conversation. "They wouldn't be the fine individuals they are without you."

Touched, Annika goes on. "It's been interesting without you and Carl around."

Zeb's 'how so?' look comes into his eyes and she adds, "I'm slowly coming back to myself."

Her husband frowns with wonder but decides not to pursue it this evening. He doesn't want to make any move or discuss any topic that might interrupt the peace between them tonight.

They both secretly believe their night is ending much too quickly, but when they reach Annika's car, he takes her hand and leans against the car. By now his emotions are running at a white hot burn and he can hardly keep himself off her.

Before Carl, Annika was always responsive to her husband's emotions. But during such a difficult time and with the distance between them, she's especially keen to her internal reactions to him tonight. Although she really doesn't want to, she works to keep a cooler space between them. She recognizes a growing fear that she's responding to her own 'call of the wild' as they've jokingly called her responses to him in the past.

Throaty, she says softly, "Babe, I'd better get going."

He can't stop himself and comes up with any excuse to delay her departure. He blurts out, "Carl shaved his head!"

Annika laughs from the shock of it and asks, "What? Why?"

It's Zeb's turn to apologize, "Sorry, I couldn't help myself. Maybe in preparation for a life on the lam? Who knows why Carl does anything?"

As Annika shrugs and shakes her head, Zeb remembers how damn much he's missed her. He grabs her gently and kisses her deeply.

Contrary to her best plans, Annika responds and he knows it. Zeb says playfully,

"I could slip in the back door later. Jarren and Lexi wouldn't mind."

Couples walk by and it seems to them that they are somehow on display. Annika is afraid they are about to cause a spectacle right there, which would be unbecoming of a minister and his wife. So she pulls back and shakes her head with an obvious no to that suggestion.

Zeb's enthusiasm has gotten away from him, and he tries again with his stage whisper that usually makes his wife laugh. "Or, we could hop in the back seat and engage in some heavy petting. Right here! Right now! How about it?"

"No pressure here, huh?" she says trying to discourage him.

Zeb's adolescent energy leaves him slightly embarrassed. "Just checking," he grins sheepishly.

Not wanting to drive him away completely, she offers him a carrot, "Maybe if all goes well next time, we can try for a wild date."

He snuggles up to her, "Just try and stop me."

Annika is pleased with their compromise but her husband suddenly gets very serious.

"Annika," her starts slowly, "I have something important to say before you leave."

"What's that?" she queries.

His voice sounds somewhat pressured, but he continues in measured tones. "I've had some time to think and I'm getting back on track, too. I was unfair to you."

Zeb has Annika's total, stunned attention. She takes in his scent, his form, every inch of him while her eyes are glued to his.

He continues, "I know now that you just needed me to listen to your concerns about Carl and the changes in our family. You did not need advice from me."

He hesitates a moment or two to think of his personal transgressions, "I was so full of myself, so filled with my own ego."

She starts to say something but he places his finger on her lips to quiet her, determined to finish.

He continues, "I wanted the folks at church to think I was a big man so I pretended to be a holy one instead. You got caught in the crossfire."

He's very serious, a side of him she's always loved but hasn't seen for a while. She stands directly before him and wipes away the tears that roll down his cheeks.

"I'm good at ducking," she comments trying to lighten the mood a bit.

"Will you ever be able to forgive me?" he asks with renewed intensity.

Annika reaches for his hand and links her baby finger with his making a child's promise. Her words provide some relief for both of them. "A to Z. First to last, forever and ever."

Bob, the psychiatric nurse from the children's unit, stands before eight adults who are sitting restlessly in overstuffed chairs spread around the homey group room.

Snacks and a variety of juices and sodas are on the table against the back wall. Several guests stand at the table filling their plates as Bob enters the room.

They take their seats as the nurse begins to speak. "Dr. Elizabeth Logan has worked with young ones with attachment problems and their families for over thirty years."

Everyone claps, perhaps out of nervousness or due to some degree of relief. Annika sits down next to her husband and listens with anticipation while Zeb just looks uncomfortable.

Bob shares, "We're so pleased to have Dr. Logan work with us. So be sure to pick her brain so you can learn as much as you can possible. That keeps her sharp."

They laugh at Bob's relaxed comments as Dr. Logan enters the room unceremoniously. She gives everyone a friendly smile and sits down among them.

The psychologist wastes no time. "Thank you, Bob," she says as the nurse sits on the edge of the group. Elizabeth begins, "You need to know you all have one quality in common, and that is you have all invested in your children. You all want them to get well and do well in life. Now you are willing to do what it takes to learn how to help them with their growing up tasks."

She looks from parent to parent. "Am I right about that?"

Everyone attentively nods and some clap, glad to know they have someone on their side, perhaps for the first time since their children came home. But others smile anxiously while others appear to be filled with sorrow.

Elizabeth continues, "Since some of you haven't been here before, please introduce yourselves and tell us why you are here."

Many of the participants in the group are also parents of the children Dr. Logan and

Annika observed in the psychiatric unit a few weeks ago.

Emma's parents, Tom and Chris, are anxious to talk and Tom starts. "Me and Chris struggled with our girl since we brought her home at three months old. I never believed little kids could get so sick so early before I lived with Emma."

Georgia, James' mother, and her ex-husband Lane are full of emotion but are at very different places today. While the father remains stone silent, Georgia speaks like she's an erupting volcano. "Oh my God, the trouble we had! James did everything under the sun and I never knew what to do with him. He's always been so naughty."

She pauses only a nano-second to catch her breath then proceeds, "He's been here for five months and is just starting to turn around. What a miracle, but I think he's still going to be a handful for me."

Lane looks completely embarrassed.

A shell-shocked looking pair, Tonya and Max are Billie's parents. Tonya looks tense and Max chews the inside of his lip. They look completely unglued and are having trouble sharing what's going on with them. Even their complexions are dark with stress and their lips are pursed.

After several moments of silence Tonya screws up her courage. "Billie is a disaster and I'm a train wreck! No wonder she's such a mess."

Max pipes up and jumps into the conversation wanting to protect his mate. "I keep telling her it's not her fault, but she won't believe me."

Tonya is certain her husband is mistaken and adds sadly, "It is my fault. My mother died right before she came to us. I got really depressed over Mom's death and couldn't take good care of her in the beginning."

There is a strained silence in the room and all eyes are on Elizabeth pleading with her to step in and save Tonya.

After what seems an eternity, Elizabeth responds, "Sometimes life strikes and hits families hard. I'm glad you're sharing your thoughts, Tonya."

The distraught mother barely breathes. "My secrets eat me alive when I keep them to myself."

Elizabeth nods to her in agreement. After that the group gives her another chance to speak, but she doesn't take it.

Uncomfortable with the silence and her own thoughts Annika speaks with trepidation,

"I understand completely, Tonya. I didn't take good care of my Carl either."

When Zeb hears his wife speaking so frankly he looks guilty and reaches out to touch her arm. Annika sits on the edge of the chair clutching a tissue.

She finally decides that she can't harbor her troubling feelings any longer. "At first I thought I hated him, but I've been so frightened of him for so long that I didn't know that I was really scared for him."

Chris doesn't hesitate to add, "That's just like at our house. I got hurt and my husband didn't see what was happening at all."

With misty eyes, Zeb joins in and says, "I didn't help when that happened in our home. I just thought Annika was imagining things, even though that's not at all how she was before we brought Carl home."

Tom perks up and adds, "Me too. Now I know that my ignoring the situation didn't help our relationship one bit."

Zeb looks somewhat relieved and nods in agreement with Tom, but Lane remains silent and looks sad and lonely and slumps deeper into his chair.

Concerned, Elizabeth invites him to join in with the others. "Lane, do you have anything to add to the discussion?"

The father shrugs and looks like he feels even lousier. The psychologist continues to encourage the group members and instructs, "If you want to know something, please ask. I want to enlighten you and help you out of your confusion."

The group chuckles out of relief from some of their tension.

Elizabeth continues, "Early childhood trauma suffered in the first thirty-three months of life, including nine months in utero before birth and two years of life, can permanently rob their children of their ability to love."

Zeb shifts in his seat but Annika is mesmerized.

"Because of an early and significant break in their relationship with their first mothers," the wise therapist goes on, "they believe they'll die if they depend on others, but it's especially frightening for them to depend on moms."

"What's the deal with mothers?" Annika asks of the group in general but hopes Elizabeth addresses the issue.

Elizabeth wastes no time answering. "An attachment disturbance becomes a mother issue. Historically, mothers protect their babies, and if for any reason she fails at that, then they are vulnerable to injury and illness."

Tonya can't wait to add, "So then these kids are mad at mom from birth?"

"They can be," the professional comments.

Tonya has more. "Why am I always the one to catch it from my foster child? I didn't abuse her."

"The damage, or trauma, occurs," Elizabeth shares, "before they develop language and since they can't tell us what happened to them, they can't distinguish between you and the real cause of their pain, often the birth mother. To them all mothers feel undependable and dangerous."

Annika and the other parents are fascinated. Lane looks like he's been shot again while Tom, awed, nearly butts in, "This is scary shit. So is that why all the mothers have similar experiences?"

Without letting Elizabeth respond, Max wonders aloud, "That's strange to me, too, but what about the fathers? Are all fathers left out, like I was?"

Dr. Elizabeth nods in acknowledgment of the fathers fears and speaks to Nurse Bob still sitting with the group, "Bob, would you like to field this one?"

Glad to participate, Bob states, "Great observation, Max. Yes, it's typical for fathers of RAD kids to relate to each other, as well. Any guesses why that happens?"

The parents in the group appear dumbfounded. Max says, "No, tell us."

Wanting to enlighten them, Bob continues, "That's a survival skill for attachment disturbed kids. They focus their primal rage on the mothers while they completely snow normally bright, sensitive fathers with their innocent looks and stories that are concocted."

Not quite ready to relinquish his educators role, Bob continues, "Think about it. What if both parents get wise to the disturbed behaviors and manipulations?" He gives the parents time to ponder the question. "We've noticed that once fathers truly see what's happening to their wives, something always changes. Either kids get treatment and the family gets better together, or the children are removed from the home because their manipulative behaviors no longer work or are acceptable."

Elizabeth adds, "Fascinating, isn't it? This disorder is a relationship problem so the prognosis varies from child to child, depending on degree. In general, those with fewer symptoms have milder forms and when treatment starts early they can often do well with their families. But children with more severe cases, or those who get treatment late or not at all, often aren't very successful in their homes."

When Georgia struggles to talk she cries, and the parents nearby try to console her. Annika leaves her chair to get the distraught mother a glass of water.

Georgia finally spits it out. "I didn't want James to have a hard life! But now that we know what it is, maybe he can get the help that's needed."

Zeb reaches out to Annika and takes her hand. Tears fall down his cheeks.

Annika's anger begins to erupt. "What chance does my kid have of being happy? Carl just turned twelve and he's already locked up in juvenile hall with serious charges against him."

Both are distraught and Zeb takes his wife in his arms and holds her tight.

Elizabeth responds, "We don't know, Annika. Sadly the ravages of neglect are imprinted on their brains with indelible ink and can last a lifetime. All we can do is keep trying."

⤐ *52* ⤏

Just like he's done millions of times before, Zeb sits at his desk preparing his sermon for the next day. Usually the process is a peaceful one for him, but today is different for some reason.

Today, instead of sitting still and looking out at the wide cloud-dotted sky to get guidance, he frowns and tries to make himself focus. He knows something is blocking him, but unaccustomed as he is to this lack of inspiration, Zeb has to work to keep himself from fidgeting.

Finally, he just gives up. He shoves his chair back from the desk and sits slumped, still. With his eyes closed the pastor seems to be having a serious discussion with his Maker. Then he takes a few deep breaths and prepares to listen for the answers to whatever is going on in his head and his heart right now.

After several minutes of silent meditation the hum of his computer and printer bring him back to the moment. His eyes nearly pop open with an idea that's never occurred to him before. Determined to follow through with his thought, Zeb sits down and slides his chair back to the desk.

With fingers poised on the keys he goes to Google and then types in 'reactive attachment disorder.' Several lengthy articles pop up and he gets lost in reading the latest literature about a problem he's been hearing a lot about lately.

He recalls that Dr. Elizabeth is pretty certain that Carl has the disorder since his behaviors remind her of the symptoms she's seen with other foster and adopted kids who had rough starts in this world.

In one article titled, "How do you know if your child has Reactive Attachment Disorder (RAD)?" it cautions parents not to overreact to their children's negative behaviors. The piece said, "First, parents should not diagnose the problem themselves as this diagnose requires mental health professionals with special training."

The next article about the symptoms of RAD stated, "Most symptoms are as unpleasant as they are distinct. Twelve of the twenty known symptoms must be present to make a diagnosis of RAD." The usually contained minister gasps as he reads the new found literature and begins printing several pages of information that he wants to keep for future reference.

Another article discusses the symptoms in more practical terms and states that the disorder tends to appear in degrees and along a continuum of severity.

"In other words," he read, "if Johnny has fourteen symptoms by the age of five and Susie has seven of the behaviors by age nine, Johnny may be more damaged." It also cautions that although the disorder appears to vary in degrees, it doesn't mean any amount of attachment is pleasant or easily treatable."

To Zeb's concern one piece concludes that, "How a child responds to treatment is determined by several factors including degree of initial trauma, the internal strength of the child, how soon the appropriate and aggressive treatment is initiated."

By the end of his reading, Zeb is full of sorrow and worry for their son. He thinks about how sad it is that Carl is already twelve and how little they know about him so far.

Being a spiritual man, Zeb slips to his knees and prays out loud. "Dear God," he starts, "I know that You are the Father of us all, including Carl and me. And I also believe that nothing happens in this world by mistake, including Carl and the circumstances that motivated us to bring him into our home."

He hesitates to wipe a tear from his eye then continues, "Dear Father, this is big, too big for us alone, and I pray You relieve Carl of the pain he carries and lead us to the professionals we need we need to find so our son gets the care he needs. May I be ever mindful that You are looking over us and will lead us to victory over this formidable problem. Amen."

⮞ *53* ⮜

Together for the first time in what feels like eons to them all, Zeb, Jarren and Lexi coax Annika down the crowded aisles in the local general store. Annika thinks they have been plotting to surprise her somehow, which has never her favorite situation. But for the life of her she can't figure out what they are doing with or to her right now. Although she doesn't want to let on, Annika is interested in where they're taking her on this mysterious mission.

Feigning fear she laughingly says, "Why did I let you talk me into this?"

Working to hide the joy in his heart that he gets from surprising his bride, Zeb states seriously, "Because you really wanted to come with us. That's why."

Jarren takes his mother's arm and says softly, "Close your eyes, Mama." She balks, but because she's surrounded by all three of them, she follows her son's directions and lets them guide her down the long aisle.

When they reach their destination, Jarren parks her next to Zeb and asks her to wait a minute. He reaches into the kennel and selects a young, fluffy puppy and places it in Annika's empty arms.

Surprised, she opens her eyes to see the excited fur ball and protests, "I'm not ready."

Her husband laughs and in a voice aimed at convincing her states, "Sure you are. You just might not know it yet."

Lexi snuggles with her mother and the puppy and coos, "Look how sweet he is."

Jarren chimes in, "And we'll help with him."

Against her better judgment Annika snuggles with the puppy and smiles broadly as she checks him out. "It seems," she chides her children, "I've heard that line before."

They both wince in recognition of their former misbehaviors but hug her, thrilled to be with their mother and their father, together.

∽

A little at a time Annika discovers that she feels some relief from the doom and despair that had settled over her for the past several months. Determined to be back among the living, the previously vital woman's energy has been revived and she's getting back into the swing of life again.

Not yet ready for Zeb to return home, Annika is driven to learn to take better care of herself and to become stronger than ever. Now when Zeb and the children want to spend time with her, they almost have to make an appointment to fit into her busy life.

Annika goes into Carl's room to clean up the mess. She thinks this could be the last time because he may never come home and feels unexpectedly melancholic. As she sweeps the floor, she finds the stuffed polar bear crammed under the bed. As she examines the dirty animal, she's overcome by how much she really loves Carl. Annika falls to her knees in prayer and snuggles with the abandoned toy.

Over the next weeks Annika is frequently found out in her flower gardens in the company of her fluffy puppy she's named Willie. Lexi and her mother visit the local nursery that's full of beautiful plants and flowers that they both enjoy immensely as they catch up with boys, fashion and flowers, of course.

She and Jarren walk along the river intently talking to each other for the first time in many months. They've also been seen at the gym together where he proudly helps his mother lift weights and exercise properly.

Starting to come alive, Annika's new obsession is riding her old bicycle that she tools around on through the city streets while she takes in the sights, sounds and scents.

Annika's neighbors are so pleased to see their friend out of isolation and back to her caring self. Sitting at her favorite table in her favorite cafe in town, Annika looks free again and laughs while she enjoys the stories her friends share with her.

While working out the kinks in their marriage, Annika and Zeb spend more time together in activities they used to enjoy early in their relationship. They've been seen walking hand-in-hand through their neighborhood and on their bikes taking little Willie for a ride in an old basket on Annika's handlebars.

Jarren and Lexi think their parents look blissful again. If asked, Zeb and Annika would agree.

⇜ *54* ⇝

Looking slightly hassled, Annika returns to their home in the family car. She turns into the driveway slowly and comes to a halt several feet from the garage door. The busy woman gets out of the car juggling her purse, the dry cleaning that's covered with slippery hard-to-manage plastic, and her keys.

Before Annika leaves the car, she reaches into the back seat for several bags of groceries. She thinks about making several trips to the kitchen, but decides against it and prefers to reduce her trips by carrying too many heavy bags all at once, like she does so many times.

Annika struggles to open the kitchen door and eventually enters with her arms completely full of grocery bags. In a hurry to relieve her burden she nearly jumps into the kitchen before the door slams shut on her. Determined to get some relief, she slings the bags on the kitchen counter and rubs her arms to relieve the aching muscles.

Annika looks around and can't find him so says in a singing kind of voice, "Willie, come to mama."

Absentmindedly, she empties the grocery sacks and puts some items in the refrigerator, the freezer and the cupboards. At one point Annika props the refrigerator door open and begins tossing out old items from the frig.

So engrossed is she, the mom doesn't notice that the answering machine attached to the phone across the room is blinking, trying to signal Annika that there's a message for her.

She stops short thinking she hears her puppy whine from the other room. Annika calls out playfully, "Willie, Willie, my baby Willie." There's no response from the pup.

Unnoticed by Annika, a lean male dressed in khaki uniform pants and shirt with sturdy work boots sits stealthily on a chair in the corner of the dining room. From the backside all that can be seen is a shaved head, a muscular looking shoulder, and on his lap a struggling, whimpering Willie.

Unhurried, Annika finishes her kitchen chores and then remembers that the pup didn't come when called. She frowns and wonders if the pooch is napping or stuck somewhere so looks under the furniture and all around the kitchen.

As she walks past the answering machine she absentmindedly pushes the button to listen but leaves the room looking for her pet before the message plays. Annika enters the living room and methodically looks all around the room. She slowly walks through the dining room intent on her mission. Suddenly terrified, the alerted mother spins around to face the intruder sitting in the corner of the room.

Her face blanches but she stands stock still. It suddenly feels to her like every hair is standing on end, and every nerve ending in her body is jangling at alert.

Carl also remains very still but the sinister smile on his face widens. His left hand has a firm grasp on the subject of her search, and Willie sits wide eyed in terror.

Even in her tense state Annika notices that in his right hand Carl holds a pocket knife with the blade open and aimed at her.

Dripping with sarcasm Carl says, "I missed you, Annika."

The panicky mother swallows hard to keep the bile down as she points at the crying puppy. "Let him go, Carl. You're scaring him."

"Am I scaring you, too?" Carl asks with a hint of glee in his voice.

With a directness Carl has rarely seen Annika asks, "What do you want from me?"

A sneer curls his lip in a frightening manner as he says, "You turned me in."

Annika answers in a voice as soft and steady as she can make it, "I'm sorry you believe that."

"So you're saying you didn't?" Carl challenges.

Rather than get into more of an argument, Annika doesn't accept his challenge and reaches out for the puppy.

Carl explodes, "Say it, Bitch!" I want to hear the truth from you just once."

Trying to calm the boy, Annika answers slowly, "I've never lied to you, Carl."

With an emotional response that continues to build, he shouts, "Right! How about I love you, Carl. Or, I care about you, Carl. You're a fucking liar! You've never loved me, not for one moment."

For emphasis the boy tosses Willie at her. Annika tries to save the pooch and reaches to catch him but isn't fast enough. The puppy hits the floor with an impact that makes him cry, but then he runs from the room to hide.

Annika's relieved her pet is out of the middle of the fracas and answers Carl's charges. "That's not true," she states clearly.

Carl glares at Annika with one of his well-practiced, cold-eyed, 'I want you dead' looks. As his rage level elevates, the boy snorts as he hears the loud chugging sound of the locomotive he carries in his head.

When Carl begins making more threatening gestures toward her with his knife, she takes a chance and says, "Please give me the knife."

Sneering grotesquely he threatens, "I'm going to use it on you."

With nerves of steel, a state that's new to Annika, she retorts, "Not a good plan, Carl."

The boy encourages her with a 'come here' gesture and invites her to, "Come on and see if you can take it from me."

"This won't look good in court," Annika warns. "If you give it up without a problem, I'll fight for you."

"Fight for me?" he blinks. "Just like you have all along?"

The determined mother holds her hand out to him with a pleading look in her eyes. With amazing calm she stands her ground, "Just give it to me, Carl."

In a challenging voice Carl repeats, "Come and take it from me."

She eyes him slowly and thinks about the situation that faces her. With unusual courage Annika walks slowly toward her son determined to do whatever is necessary to keep them both safe. She maintains direct eye contact with him and continues to hold her open hand out to him.

When Annika is half way across the room Carl lets out a blood-curdling screech followed by guttural sounds she's unable to interpret. Suddenly he lunges at her intending to do harm with the knife that's clutched in his tightly clenched fist. At that moment the phone rings sending almost deafening sounds throughout the room.

Perhaps she was startled, or maybe it was calculated, but Annika jumps back just narrowly avoiding the blade as it flashes past her midsection.

Disappointed that he wasn't able to finish the job in one swift move, Carl is frustrated and a wicked fight between them ensues. Annika focuses on getting the knife from him and finds strength and agility she's never before known. But Carl flails about acting out his overpowering emotions, so rageful that he loses his accuracy with the weapon he's depended on.

They struggle trying to get the best of each other for several minutes followed by a chase through the living and dining rooms. Using ducks and weaves, Annika manages to stay just ahead of him. They both grunt out of exertion.

The pair returns to the living room where the mother unexpectedly stops, spins around and confronts her son head on. As she does Carl lunges at her. She slips getting out of his way and hits the floor with a resounding thud.

As the frenzied boy stands over her leering at the thought of getting revenge over this woman he believes to be his foe, sweat and snot pour from his face.

Unexpectedly, the phone lets out an insistent ring that distracts him. From her position on the floor and motivated by pure adrenalin and a frightening view of the deranged boy, Annika takes advantage of the moment. She locks his legs with hers and knocks him to the ground.

As quickly as the ringing began, it stops, and as soon as Carl hits the floor, the now healthy and strong Annika springs off the floor and straddles him. With Carl somewhat disoriented, she immediately pins the hand holding the knife to the floor and yanks the weapon from his clutches.

Exerting extraordinary strength that comes from deep inside her, Annika stabs the floor with the knife and breaks the blade in one swift movement. Unthinking, she grabs the blade from the floor, cutting her hand in the process, and throws it as far as she can.

Carl cries out uncontrollably as he continues to fight to win. Still bleeding from her wound, Annika maintains a hold on the boy that keeps him on the floor.

"Let me up!" Carl demands.

Annika modulates her voice to soft and almost silky, "No, Carl. I'm in charge now."

The youth continues to struggle even when the mother feels his energy ebbing. Carl shrieks in frustration and pulls against her restraining vise-like grip on him.

As Annika maintains her hold on him, her fears turn to nearly overwhelming empathy for the damaged boy she'd grown to love.

She almost croons to him, "I'm not going to hurt you."

In spite of a desire for it to be different, his demands have less punch now. The phone rings and rings again and she listens to it but doesn't loosen her grip. She doesn't attempt to answer the phone yet.

"Let go!" Carl pleads.

Finally sure of what she needs to do, Annika answers, "No, I won't ever let you go."

The boy only half listens as the crest of his fury passes. She looks directly into his half-closed yes as she consoles him. He cautiously begins to abandon his struggle.

"I'm going to help you, Son," Annika reassures the boy.

Slowly, the mother slides off the top of him but maintains a tight grasp on his wrists and keeps her legs around him. She struggles to move the two of them slowly toward the phone.

Carl states with a question in his voice, "I don't need help."

"Not true. Not true, baby boy," she says with a consoling voice.

Carl is so exhausted that moving him any distance is like dragging dead weight. He knows he's licked for now and hates it so tries to resist Annika's efforts to slide him across the floor.

Finally, with sweat mixed with the blood from her hand, Annika reaches the phone and dials 911.

Officer Smith answers, "Lincoln Police Department."

Annika speaks with panic in her voice, "Send Sullivan or Newell now!"

Smith responds definitely, "Hang on. They're on their way!"

Carl hears her plea and tries to resume the fight but just doesn't have any energy left. Both mother and son are bloody and wringing wet with sweat.

Annika slides to the wall and leans against it clutching her charge for dear life. As they wait for the police to arrive she finds herself rocking Carl ever so slightly with a gentle gesture she hopes will console him.

Finally, the doorbell rings as she hears the kitchen door slam open. She recognizes Officer Newell's voice as he calls, "Mrs. Williams?"

"Here!" she shouts with relief.

Newell comes in from the back of the house as Sullivan enters the front door with their service revolvers drawn, ready for anything. Several other officers follow them creating instant chaos.

Not yet feeling safe, Annika maintains her death grip on her son and wanly smiles at them through copious tears. In his exhaustion Carl's response is sluggish.

Officer Sullivan squats in front of the pair and relieves Annika of her grasp on Carl. He roughly pulls the boy up on his feet and handcuffs him.

Sullivan speaks to Carl and says, "I guess we'll have to lock you up tighter this time."

Newell kneels on the ground beside Annika and looks at her wounds. When he speaks, he barks, "Get the squad here, stat!"

Annika is overcome with emotions but manages to speak anyway. "I'm okay." As she sees the officers start to lead her son from the room, she calls out, "Wait!"

The exhausted mother gets off the floor, walks slowly to Carl and stands directly in front of him. Maintaining gentle, direct eye contact with her boy, she speaks softly. "I care about you." All movement in the room ceases and time seems suspended before Annika speaks again. "I love you, Carl."

"Yeah, whatever," Carl says almost softly. The boy lowers his head and turns away from his mother.

Sullivan has been watching Annika's courageous actions and as he leads Carl from the room, smiles over his shoulder. With warmth in his voice he says to no one in particular, "She is one tough broad."

As Carl exits the house Zeb enters. He panics as he sees his bride sitting on a chair covered with blood. He leans down and takes her in his arms and whispers, "Baby!"

Annika recovers her composure and is strangely calm and says, "I'd say it's been a busy day at Black Rock."

Zeb kneels down beside Annika and intertwines his baby finger with hers. With a voice full of emotion she vows, "From the beginning to the end."

Outside, several police cars and a rescue unit park haphazardly on the William's front lawn. A dozen police officers mill around as Sullivan leads Carl to the squad car. The boy willingly slides into the back seat.

Sullivan then climbs into the driver's seat and talks on the radio. "He escaped from the detention hall. Call ahead to the Regional Center; we're bringing a slippery customer back to them."

Neighbors litter the lawns on the street surrounding the Williams place. All are curious and worried.

Uninformed, Jarren and Lexi stroll down their block until they are in close proximity to their home. The siblings look at the chaos with confusion on their faces and finally realize that the police are actually at their house. They instantly run, full bore, to the front door and enter.

≈ 55 ≈

One year later...

From the road that leads to the Lincoln Regional Center Carl stands at a large window, standing with a staff member on the landing of a stairway that looks over the front driveway. He stands stock still with a look that says he's contemplating the coming event.

The boy is taller than when we last saw him over a year ago and his body is more filled out. He has a full head of well-groomed hair and his clothes are tidy.

The emerald grass is a little long while some leaves and loose flower petals have blown against the old brick building giving it a slightly neglected look. The summer scene is tempered by an unusually chilly wind.

A car drives up to the front of the building and parks at the curb. Carl sees no activity in the car for several minutes until Annika and Zeb open their car doors in unison and step out into the cool, fresh air.

Annika's hands tremble as she waits for Zeb to walk around to car and arrive at her side.

He puts his arm protectively around her shoulders and speaks quietly, "Are you sure about this, Darling?"

Annika nods with a determined look on her face as they walk toward the building.

The staff gives Carl a final nudge on his shoulder as the boy leaves his perch at the window and soon exits the building. He tugs at his jacket pulling the collar up around his ears in a coat that's almost too small for him.

Looking more mature, Carl walks cautiously toward his parents. In spite of the fact that his face shows fear, Carl doesn't take his eyes off Annika. The two maintain a gentle eye contact as she moves slowly toward the young man before her. She sees for the first time a pleasant, almost soft look on his face and in his eyes.

Carl approaches with trepidation. His hands shake and his voice quakes as he stands face to face with Annika.

"Cold?" she asks noncommittally.

The boy shrugs and says simply, "Huh-uh."

They walk together away from the building, and Zeb takes her hand as they head for the park nearby.

After several moments of walking in silence Annika reaches out to her son and places her hand on his shoulder.

Carl benignly leans slightly into his mother and sighs.

The End

About author, JANE E. RYAN

Understanding the effects of early trauma on children's lives is demonstrated in Jane E Ryan's nonfiction book, "Broken Spirits Lost Souls" and in her award-winning screenplay, "The Boarder," the basis for this novel.

As a mental health professional, Jane has observed disturbances in parent-child relationships across many cultures in North America, South America, and Africa.

Ryan lives in Grand Island, Nebraska as she prepares to film this story in Ravenna, NE. Contact her at theboardermovie@gmail.com. or ryanjane@charter.net.

Other books written by the author:

Motherhood at the Crossroads:

Meeting the Challenge of a Changing Role

Broken Spirits Lost Souls:

Loving Children with Attachment and Bonding Difficulties

Screenplays written by the author:

"The Boarder"

"Brian's Choice"

"Looking for Jane"

LaVergne, TN USA
04 May 2010
181394LV00002B/2/P